Allisen's Notebooks

6th Grade

With My Crazy Classmates, My Super Smart Sister, & Me

Dedicated with love to my
parents, my grandparents, and
my two brothers

Published by Blobfish Books

Text Copyright © 2015 by Kelsey Gallant

ISBN: 9781790705900

Cover design by Cameron Gallant (2018)
Cover images (people): MarinaMay/Shutterstock.com
Cover image (background): Zuccheronero/Shutterstock.com
Back cover image (cat): KittyVector/Shutterstock.com
The text in this book is set in KG Burst My Bubble and Janda Quirkygirl

Summary: Sixth-grader Allisen Zepetto experiences a memorable year, both
at her brand-new school and at home with her unusual family.
[1. School—Fiction. 2. Siblings—Fiction. 3. Friends—Fiction.]

Contents

Book 1: School Starts

September 5, 2005

Hello! My name is Allisen Zepetto. I just found this blank notebook when I was cleaning out my closet today. I decided to use it as a diary. I think I'll write this diary kind of like a story. I mean, I'll only write stuff that really happens, but I'll do it in story form, with narration and dialogue and everything. I think that'll be fun to look back on when I'm older. It'll be like reading a book with me as the main character.

So, I'll start with today. Today is Labor Day. School starts in 2 days. Last night, my family and I got back from a <u>great</u> vacation to my grandparents' house in Michigan. Now I have less than twenty-four hours to enjoy the rest of summer, before the start of SCHOOL.

Don't get me wrong. I like school, for the most part. It's just that it's always been a little crazy for me, so I'm kind of nervous. I'm going to a new school this year— my fourth new school in only six years. When I was really young, I was homeschooled. Then for third grade, I went to a private school (I liked it, but it was super expensive). For fourth grade, I went to public school (It was okay, but the work was too easy). For fifth grade, I went to a Fun House school.

Fun House schools are sort of private schools, I guess, except they're less expensive and they have stores, restaurants, pools, and lots of other fun things that are open for several hours after school gets out. Supposedly this is so kids can have a safe place to stay if both parents have to work all day. That was never something my family had to worry about (Dad's an electrician, but Mom's a writer so she gets to work from home), but when we heard my cousin Carolina in Pennsylvania rave about the one she had started going to, we thought Fun House schools sounded awesome.

Until Mom and Dad enrolled my sister and me at STARS, a brand-new Fun House school right down the street. It was a mess. All the classes were made up of kids of all ages randomly thrown together and given pointless assignments that were usually either too easy or too hard. There were almost no rules, so the kids were out of control. I don't think anyone really learned much there.

Mom and Dad found a different Fun House school

for us to try this year. It's called Learner's Cove. We visited at the end of last school year and it seemed really nice. The kids seem decent, the work looks reasonable, and there's a list of school rules that all make sense.

But I'm still nervous, and that's mostly because of who's starting school with me.

I'm going into sixth grade. I'm turning eleven on September 28, so I'm pretty normal for someone my age, as far as school goes. <u>However</u>... my little sister, Mirisen, is eight. She's going into 6th grade too. With me. In my same class.

As if that's not weird enough, I have an older brother, Pete. His real name is Jefferson, but he insists on being called by his middle name because Jefferson was the name of his biological dad (Mom and Dad adopted him when I was little), who apparently wasn't a good person. Pete's seventeen, and he's really rude and annoying. He won't be in my class (good thing!) but he'll be at my same school, because it goes from kindergarten up through twelfth grade (although technically the seventh through twelfth grade section of the building is called "Learner's Academy"). Pete's in eleventh grade this year, although I think he should be in preschool because he's not very smart. Anyway, I don't want anyone to know we're related, because Pete's the kind of kid who always gets in trouble and does really bad things. He even <u>looks</u> like a punk, with his dyed green hair and disgusting lip piercing.

There's one member of my family going to my school, other than me, who is normal. That's my little brother, Harrisson. He's six and going into first grade. He's never been to school before, so he's really excited.

Okay. Enough talk about school. Let me tell you about me, so you can have a little bit of background knowledge for this diary/story I'm about to write (even though the only one who will ever read it will be me). My full name is Allisen Kaylah Zepetto. Yes, that's Allisen with an e, not an o. My parents really liked the name Allison, but they already knew a few Allisons and they wanted me to be unique. So they changed the spelling. It's kind of annoying sometimes because people usually spell my name wrong, and places that have personalized things like mugs and keychains never have anything with my name spelled correctly. But overall, I like the spelling of my name, and I like that it's unique.

Here's some more stuff about me: I live in Nashua, New Hampshire. I've lived in this same house for my entire life. My favorite thing to do is write (That might be kind of obvious). I also like to read, swim, draw, play outside, and do a bunch of other things. I have long brown hair and a lot of freckles on my cheeks and nose. You already know that I'm ten and have three siblings. I also have two wonderful parents, and three cats named

Tuxio, Sniffer, and Leelee. Sniffer is my best friend in the whole entire world, but I don't have a human best friend.

Maybe that will change when I start sixth grade. Somehow I doubt it.

September 7

School! I am writing this at school. I'm in my classroom right now, sitting at a desk on the right side of the very back row. All around me, I see unfamiliar faces, except for right next to me, which is where Mirisen is sitting. We're seated in alphabetical order by last names, and since our last name is Zepetto, we're dead last.

It looks like there are 21 kids in the class. Not everyone is here yet, but that's how many desks there are. That's a lot more kids than were in my 3rd grade private school class, but fewer than were in my 4th grade public school class, and my 5th grade crazy school class.

A lot of the kids are giving Mirisen weird looks. I don't blame them. Aside from being two or three years younger than most of us, Mirisen is very short, only like 3'8 or 3'9. She looks about six. I wonder if people think she's my little sister. I mean, she is my little sister, but I wonder if people think she's my <u>little</u> little sister, like not supposed to be in this class. I'm not going to say anything. They'll find out soon enough.

September 7, later

Our teacher's name is Mrs. Banks. She introduced herself, then asked everyone in the class to introduce themselves by saying their name and something fun they did over the summer. I managed to catch a few names— Rob Lebeng (who I remembered because he has the same last name as the principal— I wonder if they're related), Sara Corey, Natalia Frink, and Joseph San something— but mainly I was too nervous to pay much attention.

My turn came too soon. "Um, hi," I began, trying to focus only on Mrs. Banks and not on the nineteen unfamiliar students looking at me. "I'm Allisen Zepetto, and this summer I went to Michigan to visit my grandparents, and I, well, rode my bike a lot and hung out with my family and stuff."

Mrs. Banks nodded approvingly, and then it was Mirisen's turn. "My name is Mirisen Zepetto, and I—"

A boy near the front interrupted. "You're in this class?"

"Yes," answered Mirisen. "And this summer I—"

"How old are you?" a girl near us asked.

I felt sorry for Miri. I could tell she didn't want a big fuss about her age. "Eight years and ten months," she mumbled. "Anyway, since Allisen is my sister, we did most of the same——"

"Did you just say you're <u>eight?</u>" someone blurted.

"<u>Yes!</u>" Mirisen answered, trying not to sound impatient. "This summer I visited my grandparents and I read and I played with my little brother and..."

"Did you skip a grade? Or two? Or three?" a girl interrupted her again.

Miri looked uncomfortable. "Actually, I——"

Someone else started to say something, but they were cut off by Mrs. Banks. "Ladies and gentlemen, you are being very rude right now. I can assure you that Mirisen is supposed to be in this class, and I expect you to treat her like you would any of your other classmates——with <u>respect.</u>"

She let Mirisen finish, and this time no one interrupted her. But by the time we moved on to our first subject (math), people were still staring.

<u>September 8</u>

2nd day of school. My only friend is my sister. Apparently some boys in our class (particularly two class clown types named Thomas and something like Steve Ray) think it's hilarious that Mirisen is only eight, and keep asking her how old she is just to annoy her or hear it again or whatever. She told them the first couple times, then decided to ignore them. She told me she's going to calculate how old she is in days and tell them the answer in days if they ask her again.

Mirisen and I have been sitting together at lunch, just the two of us, away from everyone else because we don't have any friends yet. Actually, Mirisen does have a couple friends, because she went here for a few extracurricular activities last year, but they're all in lower grades. Fifth, sixth, seventh, and eighth graders eat lunch together, and her friends are all in third and fourth.

Today, we made the mistake of sitting at a table that later became populated with a bunch of rowdy 8th grade boys. They were all talking about... Pete.

"Yeah, this dude in my brother's math class, his hair's bright green. Bright as a traffic light. And he's got this spike through his lip and everything. He's sick."

"Hey, I think I've seen him! Yeah, scary dude. Pretty sizzle, though."

"Yeah, he's cool."

Mirisen and I didn't dare look up throughout our entire meal. We didn't even speak. We were so relieved when lunch ended.

September 10

Ah, the weekend. Two days to recuperate before I have to go to school again. Yesterday was just as yucky as the first two days.

September 11

4 years ago, terrorists flew planes into the World Trade Center in New York. Today, our church had a special peace pole dedication in memory of all the people who died in those attacks. Other than that, we didn't do much today.

September 12

School again. At lunchtime, Mirisen and I sat at a vacant table. Someone else plopped down across from us. It was a girl I'd seen a couple times at church, including at the peace pole dedication yesterday. She had blond hair and an unusual-looking face. I don't really know how to describe her face except that it looked different from most people's faces.

"Hi!" she said with a smile. "I know you from church. What'th your mane?"

Her speech was slurry and kind of hard to understand. "My...name?" I said, to make sure I understood what she was asking.

She nodded.

"Allisen, and this is Mirisen, my sister. What about you, what's your name?"

"Mouthie!"

"Mouthie?" I exclaimed. What an odd name.

"No. Mou-thie." She said it the exact same way.

"Mousie?" asked Mirisen.

The girl giggled. "No, thilly! My—mane—ith—MOUTHIE!"

"Oh!" Mirisen suddenly exclaimed. "Nowcie?"

"Yeth! Yeth! Mouthie! I'm ten. How old are you?" They began talking, but I could barely understand anything Nowcie said. I still don't know how Mirisen managed to get Nowcie out of Mouthie.

September 14

Oh, great. Does Mom want me to go crazy??? She signed me up for a typing class! It starts next Monday (Sept. 19). At least Mirisen will be in it too. Still, it goes AFTER school! That means another hour of being at school! No! NO! NO!

Mirisen's excited (of course). She'll finally learn to type really fast like Mom. Mom writes self-help books for adults as her career, so she can type really fast. What I don't get is if she's such a great typist, why can't she just teach us herself?

Oh, sigh. I guess school this year is better than it was last year, but not by much.

September 16

"I love school." That was Harrisson. He, Mirisen, and I were sitting in my bedroom. I was doing my homework and they were playing with stuffed animals (Mirisen, of course, had already finished all of her homework). "Don't you just <u>love</u> school?" Harrison continued. "I do. First grade is really fun. My teacher's Miss Enshaw. She's nice. Do you think your teacher is nice?"

"No," I answered immediately. "She gave me a 90 on my spelling test!" A 90 is an okay grade for me most of the time, but not on spelling, my best and favorite subject.

"Well, you <u>did</u> miss two words," pointed out Mirisen, who, of course, had gotten a 100. "She didn't 'give you' a 90, you gave yourself a 90."

"But she didn't even give us a word list to study!" I seethed.

"There you go, then. A 90 without studying is a pretty decent grade."

Little smarty-pants. She chose not to point out the fact that <u>she</u>, two years younger than me, got a 100 without studying.

<u>September 19</u>

Oh no! Typing class today! I am dreading having to spend an extra hour at school.

<u>September 19, later</u>

There were only three kids from my class who went to the typing class, other than Miri and me. Two of them were Toby and Mariah, who I knew were already best friends with each other. The other was Emalie Maye, a tall brown-haired girl who didn't seem to have any special friends in the class. She came and sat down next to me. After the instructor, Mr. Ellesagonan (he told us to just call him Mr. E), explained things to us and got us set up with the typing games, Emalie Maye turned and started talking to me. "You're Allisen, right? I'm Emalie Maye. Are you new here? I'm new. I used to go to a public school but my parents said this school has more options for classes and stuff so they signed me up here. I love this school! It's really fun!"

She was super talkative, and I liked her at once. I told her all about how bad my first couple days had been, about Pete and his craziness, and about Nowcie, who hadn't eaten lunch with us since last week but had waved excitedly to me when I saw her in the hallway yesterday. "Oh, I know who you're talking about!" Emalie Maye exclaimed. "That's Nalcie Halls. She ate lunch with me once too. She's really nice, but did you find it hard to understand her? I did. I think she has some sort of disability. The teacher she was with said she's in a special ed class. Hey, you wanna eat lunch with me tomorrow? I don't mind eating alone or with random people like Nalcie, but I just thought it would be fun to sit with someone from my class."

"Sounds great!" I replied, ecstatic. Then Mr. E came over and told us to stop talking and start typing.

September 22

Well, now that I have a friend in my class, school isn't too bad. Emalie Maye and I have been eating lunch together for the last couple days, and we're becoming really good friends! Nalcie ate with us yesterday too, and I had an easier time understanding her this time. And the day before yesterday, Mirisen managed to find her friend Michael Caxzis, who's in 5th grade. He's actually homeschooled, but he comes here sometimes for the restaurants and stores and stuff. When Michael's not here, Mirisen hangs out with Emalie Maye and me, which I think works out well. I still get time with my sister at school, but I also get time alone with my new friend!

Guess what. Only six days until my 11th birthday! I'm going to ask if we can celebrate with Emalie Maye.

I think school will be good this year.

Book 2: Me, A Babysitter?

September 28

Yay! Today is my eleventh birthday!

Harrisson woke me up at six in the morning by jumping on my bed. "Wake up, Allisen. Wake UP, Allisen! You're eleven years old now! It's your birthday!"

Then I heard another voice. "Technically, she's not, because she was born at 10:45 a.m, not 6:02." It was Mirisen, standing next to my bed.

"What are you guys doing up so early?" I asked them. "We don't have to get up for school for another hour at least. More importantly, why did you wake ME up this early?"

"We wanted to give you a birthday surprise!" exclaimed Harrisson.

"Nice surprise," I grumbled. "But I'd rather have my extra hour of sleep."

"Mommy's making cupcakes!" Harrisson sang temptingly.

That got me up. I went out into the kitchen and helped Mom finish making the cupcakes. Later we frosted them and I brought them to school to share with my classmates.

September 29

Yesterday, after school, I got to invite Emalie Maye over! We played for a while with my Littlest Pet Shop animals, then we got to go out to dinner with my family! We went to T-Bones, my favorite restaurant, and had some really yummy food. Then we went home and I opened my presents. Emalie Maye gave me a cute stuffed monkey! From my parents I got a pair of ice skates, a green sweater, some Littlest Pet Shop animals, and two books. I wanted to have Emalie Maye sleep over, but my parents said that since it's a school night, that probably wouldn't be too good. Oh well. Maybe some other time!

October 1

Mom and Dad just gave us some NEWS today. Mom, Mirisen, Harrisson and I are going to New York for a week! One of Mom's books is being released, and her publisher is throwing a huge party/celebration thingy, and she's going to be interviewed by TV people and stuff like that. Dad can't come because he has to work, and Pete isn't coming because... well, he's PETE. Crazy, rebellious, 17-year-old brother... yeah, not such a great idea to bring him to New York with us. He'd probably try to steal the spire off the Empire State Building or something. So, fortunately, he's staying home with Dad.

I was really excited that we'd get to travel, and go to New York, where I've never been, and take some days off school (I like school now, but a vacation's always nice!). But then Mom said something ELSE.

"Part of the time we're there, the four of us will be able to go around and visit places, sightsee, and things like that. But there will be times when I'm going to have to be in conferences or interviews, and during those times I'm not sure if you guys will be allowed to come. So during those times, we'll find a nice room in the building I'm in, and you three will stick together and do your schoolwork there until I come out."

"Schoolwork?" I asked.

"We'll have your teachers give you the work beforehand so you don't fall behind." Mom explained. That made sense. If we got stuck, she could help us (after all, she used to homeschool us when we were little, so she <u>can</u> teach). It would've been fun to not do any schoolwork while we were on vacation... but I guess I'd rather do work on my vacation than have double that when I get back!

But then Mom said the part that really got me. "When I'm in meetings, I'll need the three of you to stick together. Allisen will be in charge. Mirisen and Harrisson, if you have any questions about what you can or can't do, ask her. If you need help with your schoolwork, ask her. Whatever you need, Allisen is in charge. You won't be able to call me because I'll have my phone off during the meetings."

"What?" I squeaked. "I'm in charge? Like a babysitter?"

Mom nodded.

"But I'm only eleven years old! I just _turned_ eleven! I can't... they won't listen to me!"

At the same time, Mirisen was protesting, "But what if Allisen and I are both stuck on the same question in our schoolwork? We're in the same grade, Mommy."

Harrisson added, "Allisen can't be a babysitter. She's our sister."

"Allisen is very mature for her age, and I'm sure she'll be an excellent babysitter. You two will need to behave for her," said Mom, looking more at Harrisson than Mirisen.

I'm not so sure. I mean, I know it'll only be for a couple hours at a time, but... no Mom or Dad to look to if anything goes wrong? _I_ have to be in charge of my siblings? What if I make the wrong choice?

October 4

I told Emalie Maye about the trip and she thought it sounded awesome. Even the babysitting part. "It's no big deal. I watch Jeff Peter all the time." Jeff Peter is her little brother, who's Harrisson's age.

"Well, I've never watched my siblings, and I'm kind of worried."

"Why are you worried? You guys get along, right?"

"Yeah..." I couldn't explain my worries. I guess it's just weird to me. Mirisen and Harrisson aren't <u>little</u> kids, they're eight and six! They don't see me as an authority, especially Mirisen. I mean, really, Mirisen and I are in the <u>same</u> <u>grade</u> at school! And she's way smarter than me and knows it, so why would she want to listen to me? And Harrisson already said I'm not a babysitter... I don't know. I'm just scared, that's all.

October 8

Packing day. Tomorrow we leave for the trip. We've already loaded up the van, so once Mom picks us up from school tomorrow, we're heading straight to New York! I'm super excited and also super nervous (the nervousness comes from the babysitting part).

October 9

We're driving now! We've been driving for an

hour, which means we have about three left. I miss Dad and the cats, but I'll see them again in a week! Right now, Mirisen's reading and Harrisson and Mom are playing the game where you try to find license plates from different states. I think I'll join in.

October 10

Last night, we got to our hotel. It is NICE. It has a HUGE indoor pool with a waterslide! And our room is really fancy, with a mini-kitchen and two queen-sized beds (Mirisen and I are sharing one, and Mom and Harrisson are sharing the other). And guess what! Some of the conferences are going to be <u>at</u> the hotel! So we can go swimming while Mom's in them! Of course...I'll still be in charge, so, yikes. But it should be fun.

Last night we all hung out at the hotel together and then went to bed. Today, Mom still didn't have any meetings (maybe because it's Columbus Day?), so we got to explore the city. We went to the Empire State Building and it was sooo cool! Really high up with a great view of the city. Mom took some pictures so we can show Dad when we get home.

October 11

AAAAA! First babysitting job today. It wasn't in our hotel; it was in some other random building. Mom was in one room, with a bunch of other book people, and the three of us kids were in the room next door doing our schoolwork. Well, Mirisen and I were doing our schoolwork. Harrisson decided it would be more fun to dance around the room and sing the Lion King song "I Just Can't Wait To Be King" at the top of his lungs.

"Harrisson, can you <u>please</u> be quiet?" snapped Mirisen, who was scrunched over the page of math problems we were working on together. There was one problem on the page I didn't understand at all, and she was trying to see if she could figure it out.

"Free to do it all my way!" Harrisson sang in his loud, off-tune 6-year-old voice.

"<u>You're</u> <u>not</u> free to do it all your way. Allisen's in charge." Mirisen shot me a pleading look.

"Harrisson, please be quiet. Don't you have any worksheets to do?" I asked.

"Finished them," said Harrisson, before belting out the chorus.

"Well, Mirisen and I haven't finished ours. So, could you, I don't know, maybe draw or something?"

"I wanna sing."

"Well, we can't concentrate with you singing." I felt panic rising in me. What if he didn't stop singing, and Mirisen got really mad at him, and they got in a fight... Mom had already said we couldn't call her...

"Can I go in a different room and sing?"

"No, Mom said we had to stick together."

"Then we can <u>all</u> go in a different room and I can sing," Harrisson flashed me an adorable little-kid smile that was clearly supposed to make me be won over by his cuteness and change my mind.

"That doesn't even make any sense," Mirisen scoffed. "If we <u>all</u> went in a different room, we'd still hear your terrible singing."

"It's not terrible!"

"Hey!" I exclaimed. "Guys, listen. I'm the one in charge, and I say, Harrisson, please just stop singing and be quiet and let Miri and me finish our homework. When we're done, you can sing all you want. Okay?"

Harrisson scowled. I thought he was going to disagree, but he said, "Oh, <u>fine</u>," and slumped down in a chair.

The end of Mom's meeting could not come soon enough.

<u>October 12</u>

No babysitting today! Mom took us to the Statue of Liberty. It was really neat. We got to take a boat out to it and everything. We even tracked down our ancestors on Ellis Island! It was a cool day.

<u>October 13</u>

Blaaaaaaaaah. Today was my second babysitting job.

The meeting was at the hotel, so we didn't have to go anywhere. Mom said we could go to the hotel pool, as long as we took the room key, stuck together, and stayed safe. When she left for the meeting, we were in the hotel room.

The moment Mom left, Harrisson exclaimed, "Everyone get your bathing suits on! Let's go swimming!"

"Not right now. I'm at a really good part!" Mirisen was lying on the bed she and I shared, reading a book.

"But you _always_ read. I wanna swim." That was Harrisson.

"We've been swimming every night. We can swim tonight too, when Mom's back."

Harrisson looked at me with pleading eyes. "Pleeeeeeease, Allisen? Can we go swimming _now_?"

It was hard to decide. I really wanted to go swimming, but I wasn't sure I could trust myself to watch both of them at the pool. I mean, I wanted to be able to do my own stuff, like handstands and lap swimming and going off the waterslide, without having to be a supervisor as well. So I kind of thought it would be better to wait until Mom got back so she could supervise and I could just do whatever I wanted.

BUT that would mean listening to Harrisson complain and whine for the entire two or three hours Mom was in the meeting, and I wasn't sure I was up for that. So I finally said, "How about we all get our bathing suits on and go down to the pool. Mirisen, you can bring your book down and read it on the pool deck."

"But I don't want it to get lost, or... come on, <u>please</u> can we just wait for like ten more minutes? Just so I can finish this chapter?"

I said yes. Harrisson and I changed into our swimsuits, and played I Spy until Mirisen was finally ready about twenty minutes later. Then we all went down to the pool.

"What are we going to do with the room key while we're swimming?" Mirisen asked.

I hadn't thought of that. It wasn't attached to a wristband or anything, and of course my bathing suit didn't have any pockets. Plus it was a card key, and I wasn't sure if card keys even worked once they got wet. They probably did, but I didn't want to take any chances. We finally decided to store it in one of our shoes on the pool deck.

We were just getting in the pool when I realized we didn't have any floaties for Mirisen and Harrisson. They hadn't been using floaties during the times we'd gone swimming with Mom, but I wasn't worried about them drowning then because Mom was there. But Harrisson can't swim very well, and Mirisen's really bad at anything athletic, which means she probably can't swim either. Plus both of them are shorter than four feet tall, so neither of them could go out very deep without the water getting over their heads.

I started panicking for a few seconds before realizing that there were lots of adults around— a mom with her little girl over in the shallow end, an older man doing laps, and a couple relaxing in lawn chairs (or whatever that kind of chair is called at an indoor pool). If anything happened, I could yell for one of them to help.

We started by going off the waterslide a bunch of times. The water at the end of that is only three feet deep, so Miri and Harry could stand in it. When more people came into the pool area and the waterslide started getting too crowded, Harrisson wanted to jump into the deep end and have me catch him, the way Mom did last night. "Umm, I don't think I'd be able to catch you," I told him. "We'd probably both go underwater and sink."

Helpfully, Mirisen suggested for Harrisson to jump into the shallow end water (three feet deep), and Harrisson agreed to that. While he jumped in, Mirisen and I practiced underwater handstands. It was kind of hard for me, since the water was so shallow that my legs were almost entirely out of the water and it was hard to keep my balance. But it was fun!

The later it got, though, the more crowded the pool became. When a bunch of crazy older kids (who kind of reminded me of Pete) came and started yelling and doing cannonballs into the deep end, I decided it was time for us to leave.

"But I don't want to leave!" Harrisson protested when I said it was time to go back to the hotel room.

"Just do what Allisen says for once," Mirisen said, looking disdainfully over at the rowdy teenagers. Harrisson grumbled, but he got out of the pool.

I went over to the towel rack to get us some towels, but the shelves were all empty. Great. There were some used ones in a bin next to the rack, but they were already wet from (duh) being used, and drying off with towels that had just been used by random people seemed really gross anyway.

"I'm c-c-c-c-cold!" chattered Harrisson, shivering.

"Me too," said Mirisen.

I really couldn't think of anything to do. We hadn't even brought down clothes or anything we could use as towels, because all of our changing had taken place in the hotel room.

"What are we going to do without towels?" Mirisen asked me.

I was considering just staying in the pool until Mom came to get us. But the teenagers were being really rough and saying a bunch of bad words. I didn't want Harrisson around that. I didn't want any of us around that, for that matter.

"Uh... I guess we'll just have to go back to our

room like this." I responded.

"Sopping wet?"

"Yep."

"Are we supposed to?" Harrisson looked worried.

"Probably not, but what other choice do we have?" We exited the pool area and made a mad dash toward the nearest elevator. We jabbed at the buttons until finally the doors opened. A couple of adults got out, staring disgustedly at the three kids in swimsuits, dripping water everywhere. We ran in, and the elevator left while they were still staring.

Once in the elevator, Mirisen started giggling, and then Harrisson and I did too. We giggled all the way up to our floor, and even more when we got off and a couple more people walked by us. We ran to our room and let ourselves in. Finally, we were able to get dry and change our clothes.

October 14

Well, I'm really glad I don't have to babysit today. We told Mom about the whole pool fiasco and she laughed and said, "Well, at least it all turned out okay."

Today we got to go to Central Park and walk around the city. We also went to FAO Schwartz, the cool toy store! And when we got back to the hotel, Mom helped us with our schoolwork. We ordered pizza for dinner. It was a great day.

Tomorrow, though, I'm going to have to babysit again, and it's not going to be at the hotel. Grrr... I'm not looking forward to this.

October 15

Hey, I think I'm getting the hang of this baby-sitting thing! During Mom's meeting, my siblings and I just did our schoolwork and then made silly sketches of each other in a notebook I'd brought along. And guess what! I was supposed to have another babysitting job tomorrow, when Mom's getting interviewed, but she said that the three of us kids can go to the interview, and possibly be interviewed as well! I'm excited!

October 17

Wow, I can't believe it's our last day here. We'll be leaving in a couple hours.

Yesterday was really cool. We got to go out to dinner at this AMAZING restaurant that was set up to look like Mars! I'm not kidding! It was red-tinged inside and we rode a "spaceship" to get there, and it was just sooooo cool! And then after that, we rode a LIMO to the place where Mom was getting interviewed! It was a pretty small one, not one of those huge ones I sometimes see driving on the highway and stuff, but still pretty exciting! When we closed the shades on the windows and on the part connecting us to the driver, it felt like we were driving in a big rock.

When we got to the studio, Mom sat in a big, cushiony chair and the interviewers asked her some questions about her new book, <u>How Best to De-Stress</u>. We all sat behind the cameras and had to be really quiet, and for once, even Harrisson was quiet! Then they had the three of us come on with Mom and tell our names and ages and something important we'd learned from Mom. That was kind of hard, because there's so MUCH I've learned from Mom that it was really difficult picking just one thing. But I finally said, "My mom taught me to be responsible and to take care of people."

Today Mom doesn't have any meetings, so it's pretty much just cleaning up and packing our stuff and then (hopefully) going swimming before we have to check out of the hotel. This time we'll bring some extra towels down from our hotel room—just in case!

October 17, later

Home again, home again. It's great seeing Dad and the pets, because I missed them a lot! (not so much Pete, though). It's also kind of a bummer, because I miss getting to do exciting stuff every day and swimming in that great pool with a waterslide. And, of course, tomorrow is a Tuesday, so it's back to school. But I'm looking forward to telling Emalie Maye all about my vacation and how the babysitting went. It really wasn't that bad! I'd do it again.

Okay, it's dinner time. Dad made shish-ka-bob on the grill!

Book 3: Moving Time

October 24

I'm so excited. Only one week left until it's Halloween! Today I brainstormed costume ideas with Emalie Maye, since she's my BEST friend in the world (other than Sniffer). Usually I have my costume picked out way before now, but the whole New York trip kept me really busy and focused on that, so Halloween wasn't exactly top on my mind.

"We should dress up in costumes that match with each other, and then go trick-or-treating together," said Emalie Maye excitedly. "Like we could be a fork and a spoon. Or a mouse and a piece of cheese. Or a horse and buggy or something."

"How would we dress up as a horse and buggy?" I asked curiously.

"Oh, I don't know, it was just a suggestion. Or

maybe we could do characters, like SpongeBob and Patrick. Or Bart and Lisa or something."

"Who are Bart and Lisa?"

"From the Simpsons. Don't tell me you've never heard of the Simpsons."

I'd heard of them, but I'd never watched the show. I decided not to tell her I'd never watched SpongeBob either.

"I like your fork and spoon idea," I told her.

"Yeah, that'd be great. But how would we do it?"

We brainstormed some more and decided we'd go as a fork and spoon, and make our costumes out of cardboard spraypainted silver. We have a week to do it. I'm so excited!!!

October 26

Today I brought some cardboard I found in my garage to school. Emalie Maye brought some too. We stayed late after school (School itself gets out at 3, but all the stores, restaurants, and play and study areas are open until like 8 or 9 at night). We found an empty room where we could work on our costumes. Emalie Maye brought duck tape and scissors, and we spent about an hour trying to cut out the shapes of our costumes before our parents came to pick us up. We didn't get very far because it was REALLY hard to cut the cardboard with scissors.

When I told Dad about that, though, he said he has a razorblade that he can help us use, and that Emalie Maye can come over to our house tomorrow to keep working on the costumes! Yay!

October 27

NOOOOOOOOOOOOOO!!!!!!!! I got some <u>TERRIBLE</u> news today. It started out as a really fun day. Emalie Maye came home with me, and after Dad had helped us cut out the shapes of our costumes, we went into my room and tried to figure out how we would attach them to our bodies for trick-or-treating. "This is so fun!" I exclaimed while we were working. "We should do this next year too! What should we be next year?"

Emalie Maye remained quiet, which was really unusual for her. "What is it?" I asked, worried.

She didn't answer at first. Finally she said, in a very quiet voice, "I won't be here next year."

"What?" I was confused. "What do you mean, you won't be here next year?"

She shook her head. "I—I—I won't be here. I'm moving."

Suddenly it felt hard to breathe. "You're changing schools?" I asked hopefully. At least if she changed schools but still lived in the same town, we could still see each other.

But she shook her head again. "I'm moving to

Arizona. My dad's job is transferring him. I didn't want to tell you yet... I just found out a couple weeks ago... but... yeah."

I felt like everything was swirling around me. "You're moving to <u>Arizona</u>?!?!?!?!" I exclaimed, horrified. "But——but——when?"

What she said next was even worse: "November twentieth. That's when we have to be out of our house. We've already bought one in Arizona and everything."

I stared at her. "November twentieth of <u>this year</u>?!?!?!?"

She nodded glumly. "Yeah. I don't really want to move, but..." she shrugged.

The rest of the day wasn't that fun. I kept thinking about Emalie Maye moving in less than a month. In only 24 days. Why does my best friend in the whole entire world have to MOVE? Why can't it be somebody else? I wouldn't mind so much if it was some other kid in my class, but <u>Emalie Maye</u>?

October 29

It's Saturday, and that means I won't be seeing Emalie Maye for two whole days! Grrrrr. We got our costumes basically done yesterday, so now over the weekend hopefully we can get our parents to buy some spraypaint and spraypaint them. But I'm still SO SO SO sad and upset and mad about Emalie Maye moving.

I got in a fight with Mirisen today, which is weird because we pretty much never fight. But she said, "Emalie Maye is so lucky to be getting out of this place."

"Lucky?" I exclaimed. "She is not! It's horrible that she has to move!"

"Yeah, for <u>you</u>. But <u>she</u> gets to go live in a different place with entirely different people who she doesn't even know. I wish it were <u>us</u> moving instead."

"That's crazy!" I exclaimed. "Then <u>we'd</u> be the ones living in a different place with people we don't know! It was hard enough starting a new school this year, and now my best friend, who also happens to be my <u>only</u> friend, is moving away and I'll have to start all over!"

"<u>You're</u> lucky. I wish all <u>my</u> friends would move away and <u>I'd</u> have to start all over."

That was such a mean and oblivious thing to say that I just yelled, "You know what? <u>You</u> don't have a clue what it's like. I wish all your friends would move away too because then maybe you'd understand what I'm going through!"

I feel really bad now, because I shouldn't have yelled at her. And also, I think it's weird that she wants all her friends to move away. It's not as if she's some typical eight-year-old who might not even understand what that means, because she's a super-genius who's in sixth grade with me. So I just don't get it.

October 31

"Happy Halloween!" That's what I said to Mirisen and Harrisson when I met them in the kitchen this morning. I decided to at least try to be in a good mood for the holiday.

Harrisson smiled and said, "Happy Halloween to you too, Allisen!"

Mirisen just scowled at me, then said in a haughty voice, "Allisen, the proper way of informing us of the present holiday is 'All Hallows' Evening;' however, over time, society has shortened it to form the contraction 'Hallowe'en'."

Mirisen sometimes talks like that when she's crabby or annoyed about something, all super-smart and know-it-all-ish and everything.

"Whatever," I said. "Harrisson, is your, um, 'Hallow eve' costume all ready for tonight?"

"Yep!" exclaimed Harrisson, at the same time as Mirisen said, "Honestly, Allisen, it's <u>All Hallows' Evening</u>, not <u>Hallow Eve</u>."

I don't know what has gotten into Mirisen lately. She's had a really bad attitude these past couple weeks, and if anyone should have a bad attitude it should be me because <u>my</u> best friend is moving away.

October 31, later

Emalie Maye and her brother, Jeff Peter, came

over for dinner! We had spaghetti and meat sauce. Then we all changed into our costumes and went trick-or-treating with Dad (Mom stayed home to give out candy).

Our fork and spoon costumes looked great. Dad was able to spraypaint them yesterday morning, so they were nice and shiny and silver. We duck-taped the structures to our backs—the spoon for me and the fork for Emalie, because she's taller—and Mom took our picture. Then she took a picture of all of us kids together.

Harrisson was dressed up as a spaceship, and Jeff Peter was dressed as Sully from <u>Monsters, Inc.</u> Mirisen, to my surprise, was dressed in my old pig costume from several years ago.

"I thought you were going to dress up as a bride," I told her.

She shook her head. "People would make fun of me," she said.

"They'd make fun of you as a bride but not as a pig?" That seemed backward to me.

Mirisen just nodded. "And, besides, pigs are clumsy and so am I, so a pig's a good costume for me."

I didn't argue. We all just went out and walked around the neighborhood, stopping at every house that had lights on, and getting all sorts of candy. When we got home, Mom and Dad checked the candy to make sure it was OK to eat, and then we got to each pick a few pieces to eat.

Throughout the whole evening, I had a blast, and it wasn't until Emalie Maye's parents came to pick her and Jeff Peter up that I remembered that it would be my last (and only) Halloween with Emalie Maye.

November 3

I went over to Emalie Maye's house today! We're trying to spend as much time as possible together before she moves. Her house is a mess because they've been busy packing everything up. Her room looks okay though. We spent most of our time there, just talking and laughing and stuff. We played a couple rounds of Scattergories, and Emalie Maye taught me a hand-clapping game, and then we looked through the random stuff she was finding in her room as she was trying to pack. We're going to try to talk our parents into letting us go over to each other's houses every day until she moves, switching off so we're at her house one day, my house the next, then hers, then mine, etc. Maybe we can even convince them to let us sleep over at each other's houses every day, and then the other set of parents can pick us up at school for the next night, and so on, but that probably won't work. It's fun to think about, though.

November 6

Ten days until Mirisen's 9th birthday. I figured she'd be excited about her birthday (for one, who wouldn't be, and for two, it would at least make her seem closer in age to the rest of the kids in our class). But when Mom asked her what she wanted to do for her birthday, she just said, "I don't really care."

"Do you want to invite any friends over?" Mom asked.

Miri shook her head. "I don't have any friends."

Mom and I both looked at her like she was crazy. "Of course you do!" I exclaimed. "What about Michael Caxzis and all those other kids?"

"They all make fun of me."

"Your <u>friends</u> make <u>fun</u> of you?" I was shocked.

"How do they make fun of you, honey?" asked Mom.

At first it seemed like Miri wasn't going to respond, but then she said, "You know Domacie Cooce?"

We nodded. Domacie Cooce is Mirisen's only friend from the crazy school we went to last year. They haven't seen each other too much since we switched to this school, but I guess he sometimes comes to our school after school hours and hangs out with Mirisen.

"What about Domacie, honey?" asked Mom.

"He... when he comes... we always have fun

together, but... my other friends..." a few tears leaked out of Mirisen's eyes.

"What do your other friends do?" I asked protectively. Come to think of it, I realized she had been eating lunch with Emalie Maye and me almost every day now. I just figured that was because Michael hadn't been coming.

"They...make fun of us," she cried, more tears spilling over onto her cheeks. "They say... they say we're in love and they make kissy noises and it's really annoying."

"Oh, Mirisen," Mom wrapped her in a big hug. "Kids can be really mean sometimes, huh?"

Mirisen nodded.

"Do they know that it's bothering you?" Mom then asked. "Maybe they think they're being funny. Maybe they're not trying to be mean."

"I don't know," mumbled Mirisen. "I want to move to Pennsylvania and live with Carolina's family."

I slipped away and let Mom comfort her and help her. I, meanwhile, took a notebook and wrote down a plan.

November 8

Emalie Maye came over to my house today and we worked on stuff for my plan. Yesterday, I asked Mom privately if we could have a surprise party for

Mirisen. She seemed hesitant at first, then asked who we would invite. "Domacie," I suggested. "And... do you think we could invite Uncle Joe and Auntie Brenda and Carolina?"

Mom said probably not, since Carolina would still be in school and Uncle Joe and Aunt Brenda would probably have to work. But it's a yes on Domacie and on the party!

Today I told Emalie Maye all about it. "I really want to cheer her up," I explained. "So I was thinking what we could do today is make posters for the party, saying 'Happy birthday Mirisen,' and stuff like that."

So that's what we did. I found two poster boards, and we decorated them and wrote 'Happy birthday Mirisen' on them, and then we took a few regular sheets of printer paper and drew Mirisen's favorite things (cats, dolphins, books) and the number 9.

"I think this party's gonna be great," said Emalie Maye. I agreed.

November 10

NOOOOOO! When I walked into class today, Emalie Maye looked upset. "They changed the date," she told me.

"Huh?" I said.

"Remember how I told you I'd be moving on the twentieth? Now we have to be out of the house by the thirteenth."

"The thirteenth? But—that's—that's only three days from now!"

Emalie nodded sadly.

Since school was about to begin, I went to my seat in the back and sat down next to my sister, who had her bangs pulled back in a headband, the rest of her hair in a bun, and was wearing one of my shirts from last year, which was waaaaay oversized for her. When I asked earlier what was with the new look, she said she didn't want her friends to recognize her. Personally, I think she should just pick new friends.

"Emalie Maye's so lucky she's moving away," said Mirisen when I sat down next to her. "I hope Mom and Dad let me move away and live with Carolina."

I began feeling a little scared. Is that a possibility? I don't think I'd be able to stand losing both my best friend and my sister.

November 12

Waaaaaaaah. Tomorrow Emalie Maye will be MOVING!!!!!! We had a good-bye party yesterday at school. It was very sad. Today Emalie and her family will be coming over to our house for dinner. I'm glad I at least get to spend some time with her, but whyyyyyy does she have to move? And she won't even get to be here for Mirisen's party, which SHE helped make posters for, by the way! We both think that's totally unfair.

November 13

Saddest day of my life. Last night Emalie Maye and I exchanged addresses and promised to write to one another. She said she'd send the first letter so she could tell me their new phone number, because her parents don't know what it's going to be yet. I gave her my phone number and she said she'd call me once they got their phone hooked up. Emalie and I hugged each other and cried for about a minute straight.

"I'm going to miss you so much!" I told my best friend.

"I'm going to miss you too!" she exclaimed, hugging me tight. "You'd better keep me up-to-date about everything going on at school," she said.

"I will. And you'd better keep me up-to-date about your new school and all that."

"I will, I will."

We hugged for another long time, and then Emalie and her family had to go home for their last night here in New Hampshire. I cried for a really long time after that. I have no idea what I'm going to do now without Emalie Maye.

November 16

Mirisen's birthday!!!! Not her party, though. I

mean, we'll have a small one tonight just with our family so it doesn't seem suspicious, but the <u>real</u> party will take place on the weekend. Oh, and good news! Carolina and her family <u>are</u> able to come!

I'm still really sad though. School doesn't feel right without Emalie. Mirisen and I are back to eating lunch with just each other most days, which isn't bad, but I still wish I had, you know, a <u>friend</u> to eat with and hang out with and everything. Sometimes when I'm sitting in class I try to pretend that Emalie Maye is just absent, and that she's coming back tomorrow, but then I look over at the empty place where her desk used to be (Mrs. Banks took it away) and feel sad all over again. And now, when we partner up for activities in class, we don't have our little threesome anymore of me, Emalie Maye, and Mirisen. It's just Miri and me.

I'm waiting and waiting for a letter or a phone call or something from her. Mom told me to be patient because they need to get to their house (which could take up to 3 days, since they're driving from New Hampshire to Arizona), then set everything up and all that. Emalie Maye might not have time to call or write quite yet.

I'm still really anxious to hear from her.

<u>November 17</u>
Last night we just had a cake and a few

presents for Mirisen after dinner. And ha ha ha, Mirisen thinks that's all there is. I can't wait until Saturday when she finds out she's getting a <u>big</u> party!

Ugh, but still no mail from Emalie.

November 18

Still nothing from Emalie! How long is this going to take?

November 19

Yay! Party time! It's 10:07 in the morning. The party will start at 2 in the afternoon. But Carolina and her parents should be arriving at any moment now! Yayyyyyy I'm so excited!!!!!!!!

November 19, later

Oh, boy, was Mirisen surprised today!!! Uncle Joe, Aunt Brenda, and Carolina arrived shortly after I wrote that last entry. Mirisen and Harrisson were playing in their room when I heard Harrisson yell, "Someone pulled into our driveway!" (He didn't know they were coming either, by the way... You can't trust a six-year-old with a secret!)

A few seconds later, I heard Mirisen shriek, "What!?!?!?!?! It's Carolina!"

Next thing I heard was the two of them barreling down the stairs yelling, "It's Carolina! Carolina's here! Carolina's here!"

I raced down behind them and we met our aunt, uncle, and cousin at the door. Carolina immediately hugged Mirisen and then grabbed her hands and started dancing around. "I don't believe it! You're <u>nine</u>, Miri, <u>Nine</u>! Next year you'll be double digits! <u>Double digits</u>! How cool!"

Based on how Mirisen's been acting lately, I thought she might say something like, "Well, technically I'm not really nine until two thirty-three this afternoon." But she just hugged Carolina back and exclaimed, "I can't believe you're here! I didn't know you were coming!"

The four of us kids hung out and played games upstairs (it was my job to make sure everyone stayed upstairs) until the doorbell rang and Mom called Mirisen down to answer it. We all went down together and saw that the kitchen was decorated with streamers and balloons and the posters Emalie Maye and I had made. Mirisen was in shock. "Is this—a birthday party?" she exclaimed. Then Mom reminded her about the door and she opened it and there was Domacie! She hugged him and invited him in, and then just looked around, amazed. "I didn't know you were having a birthday party for me!"

Then her expression changed. "You didn't invite anyone from school, right?"

"No, just Carolina and Domacie," Mom said.

Mirisen's expression changed to happy again.

"Yay!"

We had a cake from Dairy Queen, and Mirisen opened presents and we all played some games together. It was an awesome party, and Mirisen did not stop smiling. "I really can't believe you guys did this for me," she said about seventy-five times. "This is so nice. This is the best party ever!"

The entire party was wonderful. But for me, the best part came around six o'clock, when the party was winding down. The phone rang, and a few seconds later, Dad brought it over and gave it to me. "Hello?" I said.

"Allisen! Hey girl, it's Emalie!"

"Emalie!" I exclaimed. "How are you? How's Arizona? Did you start school yet? What's your phone number, anyway?"

I could hear her laughing on the other side. "Slow down, I can't answer all those questions at once! Yeah, everything's good so far. I still miss you, though…" We talked for about an hour before hanging up. I wrote her phone number down on a piece of paper so I would have it for later. Yay, now we can call each other whenever we want!

Throughout the phone call, I realized something. Emalie Maye might live somewhere else now, but that doesn't mean we'll stop being friends. We can call each other whenever, and I'm already planning to write her a <u>long</u> letter when I get the chance. I'm also trying to think of what to send her for Christmas and for her birthday in January. I don't know yet, but I do know one thing. No matter where we live, or what happens in our lives, Emalie Maye and I will always be best friends!

Book 4: The Holidays Approach

November 24

Happy Thanksgiving!!!

It almost wasn't. A happy Thanksgiving, I mean. I woke up to arguing.

"I <u>told</u> Zeke and Cracker I'd meet them at the skate park!" a voice was yelling.

"Well, we're having a family Thanksgiving dinner today, and since you're part of this family, we want you to be here." Dad's voice was calmer, but held an authoritative ring.

"I ain't part of this family! Dude, soon as I turn eighteen, I'm outta here!"

I groaned. The yelling voice belonged to Pete, of course. Pete is as much of a crazy, rebellious, weirdo lunatic as you can get. I don't really admit this to anyone, but I don't like him at all. I feel like I <u>should</u> like him because he's my brother, but he's just so wacked-out and creepy that liking him is nearly impossible. Sometimes I try to make myself feel better by reminding myself that he isn't <u>technically</u> my brother, because he was my parents' friend Maggie's son before Maggie died in a car crash when Pete was seven. But then my parents adopted him, so he's been my brother since before I can remember anyway.

"Hey, you're up!" Harrisson's voice drowned out the fighting below and I looked to see him, Mirisen, and Carolina in the doorway of my room. They were all dressed and everything already. "It's snowing! You wanna go out and play in the snow with us?"

I looked out my window. The snow was coming down pretty heavily. "As soon as I get dressed," I told them.

I got dressed, first in my clothes and then in my snow clothes, and we all went out and played in the snow until the adults called us in for dinner at 2:30. Around the dinner table, there were nine of us: Mom, Dad, Aunt Brenda, Uncle Joe, Carolina, Mirisen, Harrisson, me, and Pete. Pete kept a ferocious scowl on his face the entire time and didn't say anything throughout the entire meal. Most of the time on regular days he's either not here or up in his room during dinnertime. I don't see him much anymore.

I got to say the dinner prayer, and then we all

went around saying things we were thankful for. I said I was thankful for my wonderful family and that Emalie Maye and I can still keep in touch.

The meal was great, even with yucky Pete there. I'm going to go play a game with Mirisen, Harrisson, and Carolina now.

November 27

Carolina and her family left really early this morning. They live about 5 hours away and wanted to get home with enough time for them to all get ready for school and work and stuff.

After they left, I asked Mom if we could start setting our Christmas stuff up. We like to set it up early so we can look at it and enjoy it longer. She said not today, but maybe sometime this week. I hope so!

November 29

Yay!!!!! I'm so excited! Guess what we're doing after school today! Going Christmas tree shopping! This is really exciting because usually we set up our fake Christmas tree, but Mom and Dad started talking about the real Christmas trees they always had when they were little, and they decided it would be fun to get a real one this year. It'll be so cool to be able to look at all the different options available and pick out one that's exactly perfect.

November 29, later

Why does Pete have to mess up everything? Mom and Dad made him come along to get the Christmas tree. They picked the four of us up from school in the van and we drove straight to the Christmas tree farm. Pete spent the entire ride there complaining about how he could've just stayed after school or gone to a friend's house.

"Picking out a Christmas tree is a family experience," said Mom.

Pete just rolled his eyes and muttered about not wanting to be part of our family and not caring about Christmas trees.

"It's good that you're coming, Pete, because if you weren't here, we might end up getting a tree you wouldn't like!" spoke up Harrisson from the backseat. He and Mirisen were sitting back there in their booster seats, so I had the misfortune of having to sit next to Pete in one of the middle seats.

"I don't——" Pete started to raise his voice, but caught himself. "Never mind."

We got to the farm and looked at all the trees. There were a LOT! Harrisson immediately ran to a really tall, really fat one and said, "I want this one!" but Dad said it wouldn't fit in our house.

It took a long time to choose which one we were getting. Mirisen and I really liked a fat, fluffy, pretty one, but Mom and Dad said no because that particular type of tree would make too much of a mess trying to carry it into the house. Then Mom suggested the plantable kind, but Harrisson thought all those looked too tiny. Dad found one that we all liked until we realized it had bird poop all over it. And Pete was no help at all, being rude about all the trees and saying he didn't like any of them.

Finally, I saw one that looked just about right. It wasn't too tall, but it wasn't too small either. It had no bird poop and it wasn't the messy kind. I pointed it out to my family and everyone except Pete said they liked it. We bought it and stuffed it in the back of the van, then drove home.

We set up the tree in the living room when we got home, but we didn't get to decorate it yet because the ornaments are still in the attic. Dad said he'll try to get them down tonight or tomorrow.

December 1

It's December!!!! Wow, only 24 days until Christmas. I need to start to think about what I'm giving people for presents! Let's see, I think I'm going to give Harrisson a couple Matchbox cars. I might buy a book for Mirisen, or maybe write one. Maybe I'll also write a book for my mom. Since she's an author, she loves it when we write books and give them to her. Maybe I'll

give Dad some Oreos since he loves Oreos. And Pete...
well, I probably won't give him anything. He wouldn't like
anything I give him anyway.

December 2

Dad's 41st birthday! We went to the Texas Road-
house for dinner. Mom made Pete come along, and he
groaned and grumbled about how embarrassing it would
be if someone saw him eating dinner with all of us. I
don't think he quite realizes how embarrassing it is for
<u>us</u> to be seen with <u>him.</u>

Everything was fine while we were at the
restaurant. Then we got home, and Pete retreated to
his room while the rest of us gathered around the
kitchen table to give Dad his presents. Mom called up the
stairs to Pete.

"Pete? Dad's going to open presents!"

"I don't care!" came the response.

Mom tried again. "After presents, we're going to
have cake!"

"You guys eat it without me. I'm busy."

Mom looked like she wanted to charge up the
stairs and make him come down. I knew what would
happen if she did.

"Mom," I complained. "If you try to make him
join us, there's just going to be a big fight and Pete's
going to make everyone miserable and Dad's birthday

party won't be any fun."

Mom seemed to realize I was right, because she sighed and came over to the table without calling up to Pete again. But I saw the sadness on both her face and Dad's, and it made me realize that with Pete here, we can't win. Whether he joins us or doesn't join us for something, he still manages to dampen the mood.

December 3

Today we finally decorated the Christmas tree! Pete was out with friends, so it was nice and cozy, just Mom, Dad, Mirisen, Harrisson, and me. Mom made hot chocolate and we put on a CD of Christmas carols. Dad first strung up the lights on the Christmas tree, and then we all unwrapped the ornaments and started hanging them up. I found one ornament that was a small picture frame with a picture of me, Harrisson, Mirisen and Pete in it. It was pretty old—so old that Pete actually looked NORMAL! It's hard for me to remember a time when he was normal.

When we were done decorating the tree, Mom took pictures of us three kids in front of it. Then we went and found our three cats, and each of us held a cat in front of the tree and Mom took more pictures. She said later we'll try to get one with all four kids in front of it. I don't think that'll go over too well.

December 4

Today at church we started rehearsing for the Christmas pageant that takes place on Christmas Eve. Each grade has a different part, and sixth graders are shepherds! Mirisen and I get to dress up in these cool costumes and wear shepherd headdresses and hold staffs. We also get to sing two songs: "Do You See What I See?" and "Go Tell It On The Mountain." I already know both of those songs, so it'll be really easy. And first-graders get to be sheep, which is perfect. Mirisen and I are shepherds, and Harrisson's a sheep.

What's really weird is that, on the way home, Mom and Dad were talking about the year that I was a sheep and Pete was a shepherd in the Christmas pageant! That's hard to imagine. Pete never comes to church with us now.

December 8

Snow! I played outside in the snow with Mirisen and Harrisson today. We built a couple snowmen and made snow angels and went sledding down the really tiny hill in our yard. Our driveway actually makes a better sledding hill because it's super steep, but we're not allowed to sled down it unless an adult is out on the road watching for cars.

We asked Mom to come out and watch us, but she was busy working on her newest book project. "You could ask Pete," she suggested.

The idea made me laugh. Not much of a chance <u>he'd</u> want to supervise us, or that we'd even be able to trust him if he did. We decided just to wait until Dad got home from work.

<u>December 10</u>

Christmas cookie day! We try to set aside one Saturday or Sunday in December (before Christmas, obviously) to make Christmas cookies. Today was that day. Dad made eggs and bacon for breakfast, and then we cleared off the table and got to work making cookies!

Mom and I rolled out sugar cookie dough on the counter while Harrisson and Mirisen threw spice cookie ingredients in the mixer. Dad started boiling corn syrup for his special toffee cookies. We were all smiling and talking and having a great time until... Pete came.

Pete had slept through breakfast, even though Mom had tried to wake him up. He scowled at us. "What's this? A cookie party?"

"Yep!" exclaimed Harrisson, gleefully tossing a handful of flour in the air. Mirisen rolled her eyes and reminded him that food isn't a toy.

"You can join our cookie party if you want," Mom said.

Pete made a rude face. "I can't believe you guys still make <u>Christmas cookies</u>. Christmas cookies are for little kids."

Mirisen turned around. "Well, in case you haven't noticed, Jefferson, we <u>are</u> little kids compared to <u>you</u>. I'm only slightly over half your age. Perhaps you could do something constructive with your time rather than trying to irritate us."

Pete narrowed his eyes. "Don't you <u>dare</u> call me that name! Call me that name one more time, and I'll—"

"Pete," Dad interrupted. "I agree with Mirisen. If you'd like to help us with cookies, help us. If you're just going to cause trouble and make everyone else miserable, then go do something else."

"Fine," said Pete, and, stuffing a handful of the sugar cookie dough in his mouth, he walked out the door.

Mom looked worried. "Where's he going?"

"I don't know," said Dad. "Someone watch the toffee." He left the house as well.

Dad didn't come back for a couple minutes, and then he and Mom went into a different room to talk about Pete. They didn't come back for a long time, and by then the toffee was burnt because we didn't know how long it was supposed to cook, and the sugar cookie dough was a mess because I'm really bad with the roller. We managed to fix it, but cookie day wasn't as fun after that.

Why does darn old Pete have to mess up <u>everything</u>?

December 13

Ugh, I'm getting so sick of Pete. When Mom picked us up after school, we went immediately to Wal-Mart to go Christmas shopping. Pete was just grumbling the entire time and then took out his cell phone and started talking to one of his friends. He started using such bad language that Mom took him aside and had me, Mirisen, and Harrisson go into another aisle. I tried to distract Harrisson so he wouldn't hear what Pete was saying, but Pete was being so loud that Harrisson probably heard everything anyway.

I didn't end up being able to buy anything I wanted except the Oreos for Dad. It was <u>not</u> a fun shopping experience.

December 15

Ten days till Christmas! My book for Mom is almost done. Dad's present is wrapped and under the tree. I have a great idea. I think I'll buy Harrisson's present at <u>school</u>! Our school store sells toys!

I still need to find a book for Mirisen. She likes nonfiction, science-y stuff. And I want to get something to send to Emalie Maye in Arizona. Maybe a stuffed animal or something. I can get that at school too, and then I won't have to go out shopping again except for Mirisen's present!

December 18

A week till Christmas. Christmas pageant rehearsal today. I still haven't been able to shop for Mirisen's present. Yesterday Pete's friend "Cracker" came over (I don't think that's his real name). He's just as weird as Pete, or maybe weirder. Pete was originally going to go hang out with Cracker somewhere else, but Mom and Dad said no. They said Cracker could come over here, though, so he did.

Pete and Cracker just flopped on the couches in the living room and ate a bunch of snacks and put the TV on. Then Mirisen walked by and told them they weren't allowed to eat snacks in the living room. Pete just threw a piece of popcorn at her. Then Mom walked by and said that what they were watching was inappropriate and Pete said, "Dude, we're seventeen! We can watch R movies! Just make the kids go somewhere else!"

Mom suggested that Mirisen, Harrisson and I go out and play. We did, gladly! I don't know exactly what happened after then, but a few minutes later Cracker sped off in his car, waaaaaayyyyy faster than the speed limit for our little road. And I could hear Pete yelling and slamming doors in the house.

WHY did Mom and Dad have to adopt him???? WHY can't I have a normal big brother???? WHY does he have to be so obnoxious all the time????? WHY WHY WHY????????????????

December 20

Last day of school before Christmas break! Yayyay! We had a Christmas party in my class. Mirisen and I brought in some of the cookies we'd made on Christmas Cookie Day. Some other kids brought in yummy treats too. And, surprisingly, our strict teacher, Mrs. Banks, put on some Christmas music! We were allowed to talk to people in our class and get up and dance around the classroom and everything! The only sad thing was that I kept wishing Emalie Maye was there. We would've had a blast! But I hung out with Mirisen, and then a big group of other kids invited us over to join them, so it was fun.

December 22

Today Mom got out some old photo albums and she and I looked at them together. We looked at the one from December 1995 - August 1996. The first several pages were pictures of me as a cute one-year-old, by myself and with Sniffer and with Mom and Dad and some of our other relatives. Then in March 1996, Pete started showing up in the pictures.

"This was when Pete first came to live with us," Mom said, showing me a picture of Pete, age 7, wearing Batman pajamas and holding a battered teddy bear. He looked like a cute, normal little kid—not at ALL like Pete now.

"Are you sure that's Pete?" I asked.

Mom laughed. "I know, he's very different now, isn't he?"

I nodded and tapped the picture. "I wish he was still like this."

"So do I," Mom said seriously. "I guess what we have to remember with Pete... there's no excuse for being as rude as he is sometimes, but we need to keep in mind that he hasn't had a very good life. He never had a dad to take care of him before coming to live with us, and he was just this little kid when his first mom died." She pointed to the picture. "He's made some really bad choices since then, but we need to remember that he's still a person. He still needs love just like the rest of us." Mom pointed at the ceramic manger scene we had set up on the mantel. "Christmastime especially should be a reminder of God's love for all of us. He sent Jesus down to earth for all of us... even for Pete. Maybe if we treat him with enough love and kindness, Pete will eventually come to believe that and learn how to act in love as well."

She gave me something to think about. Maybe I

will get a present for Pete after all!

December 24

Christmas Eve! Mom and I went shopping yesterday and I finally got my present for Mirisen—a book on plants. I got something for Pete too. And tonight is the Christmas pageant! Yay!

December 25

Merry Christmas!!!!!!!!!!!!!!! The Christmas pageant was excellent last night, and so was the Christmas Eve service after it. Today was super fun as well! I was woken up by Harrisson shouting in my ear, "It's Christmas! It's Christmas, Allie, get up, get up!" I went downstairs and there were a bunch of presents under the tree. Mom and Dad and Mirisen were already there. "Are we waiting for Pete?" I asked.

"Yes," said Mom.

"I'll go wake him up!" yelled Harrisson. Before any of us could stop him, he raced back up to Pete's room and we could hear him yelling "Pete, Pete, get up! It's Christmas, get up, get up!"

Mom and Dad exchanged nervous glances, and Dad headed upstairs too. But just a few minutes later, all three male Zepettos came downstairs together. Pete wasn't smiling, but at least he wasn't scowling or protesting either. I guess even Pete can be nice on

Christmas!

We opened our gifts. I got a lot of cool things, and everyone liked what I gave them. Even Pete! Mom handed him the little wrapped package and said, "It's from Allisen."

Pete opened it up with a confused look on his face. "Hair dye?" he said. "You got me Halloween hair dye?"

"Yeah," I said. "Because you like to dye your hair. And I thought you might like blue."

Pete stared at it for a couple more seconds, then at me, and then he finally cracked a tiny smile. "Yeah," he said. "I do like to dye my hair. Thanks, Al."

It was a wonderful Christmas after all!

Book 5: Why Me?

January 1, 2006

HAPPY NEW YEAR!!!!!!!!!!!!!!!!!!!!! Mom, Dad, Mirisen, Harrisson and I are all in the living room (Pete's at a friend's house, a reward for making better choices over the past couple days). We just watched the ball drop in New York City on TV. It was pretty cool to see it this year and think, "Hey, those buildings look familiar! I've been there!"

I can't believe it's the year 2006. Six whole years of living in the 2000's already! This March, Harrisson will turn seven. Pete will be eighteen in August (maybe he'll finally move out), and in September, I'll turn twelve! Then, in November (I know, it's a long time away), Mirisen will be <u>ten</u>! And—oops, Mom just told me to get ready for bed. Seeya!

January 4

Back to school after a two-week Christmas break! Oh, well. I like school. Even though my <u>best</u> friend lives in Arizona now, I actually do have a few other sort-of-friends. Sara Corey and Elizabeth Johnson and Rebecca Hanson are nice, and so are James Hinker and Rob Lebeng. And I sometimes eat lunch with Hannah Barnette, from seventh grade, or Nalcie Halls, from special ed.

Today I ate lunch with Sara, Elizabeth, Rebecca, Hannah, and one of Hannah's seventh-grade friends, Claire. Mirisen ate with her friend Michael for the first time in a while (She told her friends at some point before Christmas break how she didn't like them teasing her about Domacie. They agreed to stop, so everything's good again!). It was kind of weird not having Miri at my lunch table, since the two of us have been eating together (sometimes with other people, sometimes not) since November. But in a way it was sort of nice, just getting to interact with other kids and <u>not</u> my sister, who I see every day at home anyway. Not to sound rude or anything.

January 6

Tomorrow Dad's going to take me, Mirisen, and Harrisson to Roby Park to go sledding. Roby Park is this park near where we live, and they have an AWESOME sledding hill! Much better than the tiny slant in our yard. I haven't been there since last year. This is going to be awesome!

January 7

It was awesome. We go so fast down that hill, and I love feeling the wind whipping around on my face. I love winter! I mean, I love all the seasons, but it's hard to beat zooming really fast down a hill with cold, refreshing air hitting you in the face. I can remember a couple years ago, when we still had our dog Goldie, when we'd take Goldie to Roby park and she'd run all the way downhill with us, nipping at our mittens. Goldie died two years ago and I miss her.

Wait, why am I talking about something sad when I could be talking about something fun? Dad's taking us sledding again tomorrow after church! Yippee!

January 9

Wow, 1 cannot believe that happened. Yesterday was terrible. A terrible, horrible day.

Dad did take us sledding again, like he promised. And it started out good again. We were having a lot of fun, just like the other day. But then disaster struck.

I got on my sled for probably the twentieth time that day and took off down the hill, like usual. There were some little mounds of snow that people were using as jumps in various places on the hill. I was mainly trying to avoid them, because doing jumps on a plastic sled like I had hurts! Anyway, I started going down the hill, and then this little kid, maybe three or four years old, appeared out of nowhere in front of me. I didn't want to hit him, so I swerved my sled. I swerved right into one of those jumps and flew over it sideways. It was a big one and I felt myself get a lot of airtime before landing uncomfortably on my left arm.

My arm <u>hurt</u>. It was weird because I had wiped out a few times before, and landed on my arms or whatever, and it had never hurt as much as this did. I felt tears coming to my eyes and it took a little while to realize that I should probably move out of the way so nobody would run me over, or try to avoid me and wipe out like I had.

I picked up my sled and walked, crying, over to the edge of the hill. Moments later, Dad came rushing down from the top of the hill. "Allisen!" he exclaimed. "Allisen, are you all right?"

"My arm hurts!" I sobbed, holding it up.

Dad gently took my mitten off and rolled up the sleeve of my coat. He then started feeling my arm and asking me to twist it and spread my fingers out and things like that. "Ow!" I yelped as I tried to twist it around. I tried moving it up and down. Up was okay, but down hurt like crazy, and I wasn't even bending it far down at all. Then I tried to spread my fingers apart. Ooooh! There was a pain in my hand like you would not believe.

Dad rounded up Harrisson and Mirisen and walked me down the rest of the hill. "Guys, I think we need to take Allisen to the doctor. She hurt her wrist."

Harrisson groaned, but Mirisen looked worried. "I hope you didn't fracture your radius or ulna," she said. I was in so much pain I didn't even bother asking her what those terms meant.

We all got in the van and Dad called Mom on his cell phone. "Mom's meeting us there," he said. He sped off to the doctor's office, going at least ten miles per hour over the speed limit. It was then that I began to feel a little worried. If my arm was broken, that would be terrible! I spent most of the ride praying, "Pleeeeease don't let my arm be broken!"

When we got into the doctor's office, we had to wait for a little while, and then the nurse or doctor or whoever had me do pretty much the same things Dad had me do, such as spreading my fingers out and moving my wrist around. Then she brought me into an X-ray room, which I would've thought was pretty cool if I hadn't been in so much pain and worried that my arm might be broken. She had me wear a lead vest to protect my chest from radiation, and put my arm in an extremely uncomfortable position on the X-ray machine. She took three different X-rays, each time placing my arm in a different painful position. Then I went back out with my family to wait for results.

A different doctor came out with the results. He showed us the X-ray pictures, and then pointed to a tiny crack in my bone on one of them. "See this? That's your ulna. You fractured it."

I couldn't believe that that tiny little crack could be causing all that pain. Nor did I actually think at that time that I would need to wear a cast. When I thought "broken bone," I pictured a bone that was entirely snapped in half. But then the doctor started talking about casts, and I realized that my arm was broken.

I cried even more then. Not because it hurt more, but because I didn't want a cast. If I had a cast, I couldn't go sledding anymore. Nor could I do pretty much anything else fun. And it would probably be really uncomfortable.

A different person brought me into a different room and asked me in a cheery voice what color I wanted my cast to be. I was in such a bad mood that I just grumped, "Maroon," because I figured they probably wouldn't have maroon.

"I'm sorry, I should have told you which colors we have first," she told me. "Right now we have red, green, white, black, and I think a tiny bit of pink."

"Fine, green," I muttered.

The lady first put something like a sock on my arm, with a hole cut out for my thumb and a separate hole for the rest of my fingers. Then she put some cotton over that, and over <u>that</u> some soggy stuff that hardened after a couple minutes. Then she put the green stuff—it sort of reminded me of a rubbery version of party streamers—over that. "All right, this is all set," she told me after letting it rest for a moment. "What a pretty cast!"

It may be a pretty cast, but I sure don't feel any better about having it.

<u>January 11</u>

Oh! Torture! Two days of pure torture! <u>Three</u>, actually, if you include the 8th. Three days of pure torture!

Mirisen and Harrisson can still sled and play in the snow. <u>They</u> can still do whatever they want and have fun. As for me, I can't even build a snowman, because my cast can't get wet. When I take a shower, I have to put a plastic bag over my cast arm so water doesn't get on the cast. It's a pain in the neck, or should I say a pain in the arm! At least it doesn't hurt anymore. It did for a while after I broke it, even once the cast was on, but Mom and Dad let me have a little medicine and eventually the pain went down.

Sleeping is another thing. I usually sleep on my stomach, with my arms up beneath my pillows, sort of cushioning my head. I can't do that with my cast because then I'm lying on my cast, and I can feel it through my pillow. I have to sleep on my back, which I'm not used to. As if that's not bad enough, last night my cuddly Sniffer kitty came to sleep with me, like he often does, and he laid right on my non-broken arm (or my non-<u>fractured</u> <u>ulna</u>, or whatever). I usually pet him when he sleeps with me, but I couldn't even bend my cast arm properly in order to pet him. I bet he thought I was mad at him or something.

Mom told me to look for positive things, but so far I've only found one: at least my cast isn't an elbow one. It covers most of my hand (all but my fingers) and it goes up my arm but stops before my elbow. <u>That's</u> a good thing! I would hate it even more if it covered my elbow.

Oh, and I guess there's another thing too. It's my left arm, and I write with my right hand, so at least I can still WRITE! I would be so mad if I couldn't write. Especially because writing's just about all I can DO now.

Well, good bye.

<u>January 12</u>

Wow, this is annoying. I can't wear most of my clothes because the cast is too big to fit through the sleeves. I have to wear Mom's shirts instead, mostly, and that's annoying because they're all too big for me. Man, I hate having a cast!

January 13

My cast is covered with signatures. Mom, Dad, Mirisen, Harrisson, and even Pete signed it (Pete scribbled his name really sloppily, but hey, at least he signed it). At school, I got signatures from Sara, Elizabeth, Rebecca, Hannah, Claire, Rob, James, Nalcie, and a couple other kids (actually, I think it ended up being my entire class except for Stivre and Tomas), plus Mrs. Banks. And even though Mirisen had already signed it at home, she signed it again at school with a poem: "A fracture can sometimes seem like a curse, but out of all things, it isn't the worst." Yeah, Mirisen, easy for <u>you</u> to say. <u>You're</u> not the one who can't go sledding for another month.

The doctor told me that my cast has to stay on for five weeks total. I calculated the exact day it will come off—February 12. At least I'll have it off by Valentine's Day. I can't <u>imagine</u> having to wear a cast on Valentine's Day! Especially since it's green, and green isn't a very Valentine-ish color.

Waaaaah. Harrisson and Mirisen are going out to play. Again. I think I'll just sit here and watch them out the window, bored.

January 15

I've had my cast for a week. I'm used to it, I guess. Some kids in my church class signed it this morning. But guess what happened after church! Dad took Mirisen and Harrisson sledding at Roby Park!!! That is <u>so</u> unfair. Not that they get to go, but that I <u>don't</u> get to go! Even though I broke my arm sledding, I still want to sled!!!! Why did I have to break my arm?

January 18

Hey, Mom told me something good about having a broken arm today. My bones need lots of calcium to heal. The reason that's good news is because... calcium includes ICE CREAM!!!!! Hahaha! I don't think Mom's going to let me have double helpings of ice cream every day, but it's worth a try!

January 20

I tried seeing if I'd be allowed to eat extra ice cream every day until my arm heals, but Mom and Dad didn't fall for it. Not like I expected them to. But today, after school, Mirisen and Harrisson went outside to play in the snow and I just couldn't take it anymore. I took a plastic bag, put it over my cast like I do for the shower, and crammed my coat over it. My cast fit through the coat sleeve but not the part that my hand is supposed to come out of. That was okay, though, because I wouldn't be able to fit my mitten over my cast, so it was good that my fingers were still in my coat sleeve.

It worked okay. I could only use my right arm to pick up my sled and help build a snowman. My coat felt awkward with nothing sticking out the left sleeve. But at least I was outside!

When Mirisen and Harrisson went sledding down the small slope in our yard, I went right along with them. I wasn't able to steer to the left very well, but there wasn't really any <u>reason</u> to have to steer anyway, so it was fine. I sledded down our slope 8 times and didn't wipe out at all!

<u>January 22</u>
Two weeks down. Only three left!

<u>January 25</u>
We did an obstacle course in gym today. We had to climb over and through stuff, and do some hurdles, and all sorts of things like that. And guess what! I was able to do everything, even with my cast! My teacher said I didn't have to do all the activities, but I wanted to and was able to, so it was really cool!

I guess now that I've had the cast for a while, I've pretty much gotten used to it. I mean, I still don't <u>like</u> having it, and I can't wait until it comes off. But I can still do almost everything I could do without it, and it's not that much of a bother. And even though I have to miss out on <u>some</u> sledding and things, it's not as if I'm missing the whole winter. After all, I still have most of February and the whole of March!

Book 6: Love, Love, Love

January 31

I found out some exciting news today! My class is getting a new student! Mrs. Banks let the news slip on accident during social studies, and now she won't tell us anything else about him or her. Personally, I'm hoping it's a girl who likes to write and read and sled and swim and do everything else I like to do. I hope she's nice and likes animals and doesn't think Littlest Pet Shop and Pound Puppies and stuffed animals are babyish. I hope she's sort of athletic but not super obsessed with sports, and I hope she's not crazy about makeup or clothes. Basically, what I'm trying to say is, I hope she's the perfect friend for me.

Since Emalie Maye moved away, I've been kind of lonely sometimes. I mean, I have friends, but nobody who I can eat lunch with every day and have them come over to my house and I can go over to their house and we can do everything together. Emalie Maye is still my best friend, of course, and nobody can ever replace her. But... I could have two best friends, right? I could have one long-distance, penpal/phone-pal best friend, and one who I see every day. That would be perfect!

I'm going to pray that this new student and I will become really good friends.

February 4

Wow, Valentine's Day is in 10 days! Today Mirisen, Harrisson and I made some valentines. I usually buy a box of store-bought valentines for my classmates, but I like to homemake ones for my family. I made one for Mom, one for Dad, and one to send to Emalie Maye. I didn't make Mirisen's and Harrisson's because they were with me, and I wanted the valentines to be a surprise. And I didn't make one for Pete, because... well, he probably hates Valentine's Day and I don't really like him that much anyway. That's okay, right?

February 6

Today when I walked into class I realized that there was an extra desk in our classroom! It was in the front row, which meant that the new student's last name probably started with something close to the beginning of the alphabet (Mrs. Banks is HUGE on alphabetical order). It didn't look like the student was there yet, though.

The student actually came in during math, our first subject of the day. There was a knock at the door, and Mrs. Banks went over to open it and to talk to someone in the hallway. She came back in followed by a tall boy with reddish hair that kind of stuck up all over his head.

"Ladies and gentlemen, this is our new student, Jack Bersner," she said. "I'd like you all to give him a proper greeting."

We all said, "Hello, Jack," in the prim and proper way she'd taught us at the beginning of the year to greet people. I watched as Jack's eyes flicked lazily around the classroom. He didn't seem nervous like I would be in front of a whole class staring at me. His eyes met mine for a fraction of a second and he gave me this really weird sort of raised-eyebrows smirky cocky look. I have no idea what that was all about but I was already losing hope that the new student and I would become friends.

It just got worse. When we lined up to go to lunch, he ended up right behind me. We're supposed to be silent when we're walking through the halls, but he just would not stop talking! "Psssst!" he said. "What's your name?"

"We're not supposed to be talking," I whispered as quietly as I could. Mrs. Banks is a <u>stickler</u> on rules.

"Do you like this school?" he asked.

"Shhh!"

"How long have you been going here? Since kindergarten?"

I ignored him. At least, I did my best. It was pretty hard when every few steps he would whisper another question. Once we got into the lunchroom, I managed to lose him because he went off to get hot lunch and I went immediately to sit down. I sat with some girls from my class, and made sure to stay between Sara and Rebecca when we lined up again, and didn't have to bother with Jack Bersner for the rest of the day.

February 8

AAAA! Today Mrs. Banks told us about the Valentine's Day dance that this school apparently has every year. This year, it's going to be on Friday, February 17. That's in NINE DAYS, people!!!!!!

Mrs. Banks said that you can go by yourself or with friends or with a partner. I think <u>everyone</u> in my class wants to go with a partner. "Who are you going with, Allie?" Liz asked me at lunch.

I shrugged. "I didn't even know they were <u>having</u> a dance."

"Well, who would you <u>want</u> to go with, if you had your pick of anyone in the school?"

I thought about it. Most of the boys in our class were pretty immature and annoying, especially when it came to Valentine's Day stuff. When Mrs. Banks was talking about the dance, our "class clowns" Stivre and Tomas were making kissy noises and just being crazy, and most of the other boys in the class were laughing at them. The only ones who weren't laughing that I noticed were Joseph San Drana, Robert Lebeng, and James Hinker. Joseph is kind of intimidating—you know, the kind who always is dressed perfectly and has all the right answers and everything— and Rob is the principal's son, which makes him popular, so I imagined a lot of girls would want to go with him. So that left James.

"I guess maybe James?" I said as sort of a question.

"Ooh, <u>James</u>!" Rebecca teased. She and most of the other girls we were sitting with started giggling, and I felt my face get red because it wasn't like I <u>liked</u> him or anything, he was just one of the only sane boys in my class.

"Oh, darn, I wanted to go with James," said Sara. "Oh, well. You claimed him first, so I guess I'll have to pick someone else."

"What about that new kid, Jack? Anyone wanna go with him?" asked Melody. "He's kind of cute."

I almost gagged on my sandwich. "Cute?" I exclaimed. "He's annoying, that's what he is!"

"Really? What's annoying about him?"

I shrugged. There was too much to explain.

February 9

WOW, was I right about there being too much to explain! So, today we had library as our Special (Specials are library, gym, art, music, and computers, and we have one of them each day of the week). The librarian talked a little bit about the Dewey Decimal System and then gave us some free time at the end, in which we could just browse for books or read if we wanted.

I went straight to the fiction section and found the newest book from my favorite series, The Amazing Days of Abby Hayes. I had just sat down on a pouf and started the first page when...

"Hey, you're never gonna get a date for the dance with that cast on. You want me to take it off for you?"

I looked up to see Jack Bersner (obviously, who else would say something that crazy?) grinning obnoxiously at me. "Very funny," I said. "I'm actually getting it taken off in three days. And I'm not worried about finding a partner."

"Oh, yeah? What, you mean you already have

one?"

"Not yet, but I will."

"You still thinking about James?"

I looked up in surprise, because how would he know I was thinking about going with James? "Maybe," I said.

"Hah!" He had that cocky smirk on again. "Well it just so happens that <u>James</u> thinks you already <u>have</u> a partner. And it also just so happens that James has just asked your friend Sara to the dance."

I stared at him. Then I looked beyond him and saw Sara giggling, surrounded by Liz and Melody and Rebecca and Natalia, all of whom were giggling as well. Jack shrugged. "Oh, the wonders of eavesdropping on lunch tables."

That was <u>it</u>. "You were <u>eavesdropping</u> on us?" I exclaimed, outraged. "And, what, James was going to ask me to the dance but you <u>lied</u> to him so Sara could get a good partner and I'd be stuck with some— some immature boy who should probably be in <u>kindergarten</u>? What do you have against me, anyway?"

"Nothing!" he said, holding his hands up innocently. "Nothing against you. It just seemed like Sara <u>really</u> wanted to go with James, if you know what I mean. And you... I mean, come on, you can find somebody else."

I was trying to come up with some sort of

clever response— maybe using a lot of big words like Mirisen does whenever she's annoyed with someone— but then Mrs. Banks appeared and told us that it was time to go back to class. So I just walked off without another word to him.

<u>February 11</u>

Yay, it's the weekend. That means no Jack Bersner. I am soooo sick of that kid. He's such a pest. Yesterday my siblings and I had to stay a little late after school, because Mom was running secret errands (I think something to do with Valentine's Day baskets). Mirisen found some of her friends, and Harrisson stayed in a playplace area with some other little-ish kids, and I went off by myself to look in some of the stores and see if I could run into anyone I knew.

Well, I did run into someone I knew, but it sure wasn't anyone I was looking for! It was Jack, and he started following me <u>everywhere.</u> I went to the toy store, he followed me. I went to the snack shop, he followed me. I went to the library, he followed me. You get the idea. And every time I turned around, he seemed to be making a huge effort to make it look like he wasn't following me, just examining a picture on the wall or something. Uh-huh, right. What is that kid's problem? Does he have nothing better to do than to stalk random classmates for no reason?????

February 12

Grrrrrr. Today is the day I was SUPPOSED to get my cast taken off, but Mom said I had to wait until tomorrow because the place where she made my appointment is closed on Sundays. Why do I have to wear this thing for an extra day??? I just want it gone already!

February 13

I'm in the waiting room right now, waiting until they call my name and I can get my cast taken off. Guess what. A really weird thing happened today. Jack Bersner was actually nice! I was packing my stuff up to go home at the end of the day, and I was having a hard time doing it because I had all my regular stuff <u>plus</u> the Valentine box I made today (which I was bringing home to put some finishing touches on), and I could pretty much only hold things with one arm. Everyone around me was talking and goofing off and not paying any attention to the fact that my papers were splatting everywhere. I was starting to get panicked because Mrs. Banks would ask us to line up at any moment, and she <u>hates</u> if anyone isn't ready on time. But just then, I heard a voice behind me say, "Need some help?"

It was Jack. "I'm good," I said, because I thought he'd probably just mess my stuff up even more. But he said, "No, really, you look like you need some help with that," and started actually <u>helping</u> me! He gathered my papers from the floor and asked where I wanted them. I told him to stuff them in my math book. He did that, and then gathered all the books I was taking home and neatly placed them in my backpack. He tried putting my lunchbox in my backpack as well, but that didn't fit.

"I can carry your lunchbox or Valentine box for you," he offered. "Because I don't think you want to try stuffing that pretty box in your backpack. It'd get ruined."

I looked at him suspiciously, wondering why he was being so nice. But I eventually handed him my lunchbox (he couldn't ruin that as easily as he could my precious Valentine box) and let him carry it for me. All the way down the stairs and out the door. He even held it until Mom came to pick me up, and then he handed it to me once I was sitting down and had put my Valentine box on the seat next to me.

"Who was that?" Mom asked as we drove away.

I told her it was Jack, and she seemed surprised because I'd already told her how I didn't like him. I'm pretty surprised too.

Ooh! My name was just called!

February 13, later
YAAAAAAAAAYYYYYYYYYYYYYYY!!!!!!!!!!!!!!!!!!!

NO MORE CAST!||||||||||||||||||||||||||||||||||||||||||||||||||||||||||||||||||||||||||||||

The doctor took it off with a <u>saw</u>. I mean, an actual electrical saw, with a spinning blade, like my dad might use to cut a board or something. I was kind of scared that it might hit my skin, but it didn't. When the cast was finally off, my arm felt really weird and light. I put my two arms next to each other and my left one is skinnier than my right. The doctor said that's because my left one hasn't gotten a lot of exercise over the past five weeks.

The doctor gave me a splint that I have to wear for another week, in place of my cast. I don't mind. It's a lot smaller than the cast, so I can wear regular clothes now. And I can take it off whenever I want! It's Velcro! No more plastic bags for showers! I'm actually glad I have the splint rather than just my plain arm, because my arm feels really fragile right now, like if I accidentally bang it against something it might break again. The splint helps it feel less breakable. Oh, and the doctor also said I should start using my left arm more, not heavy lifting or anything, but just light stuff. I don't feel like I can do that yet. I really hope this weak feeling is just temporary.

But Hooraaayyyyy!||||||||||||| No more cast!|||||||||||||||

<u>February 14</u>

Happy Valentine's Day! Wow, a lot happened

today. I hope I have time to write it all before bedtime.

First of all, last night when I got home, I filled out valentines for all my classmates (including Jack and all the other annoying boys like Stivre and Tomas—the rule was, if you were making valentines, you had to make them for <u>everyone</u>). I also finished my box.

This morning, when I went into my classroom, Jack immediately saw me and said, "Oh, come on! You got your cast taken off without even letting me sign it?"

I almost said something rude like "I was never planning on having you sign it," but I remembered how nice he was yesterday and instead said, "Yep."

"I bet it feels good, right? Finally having it off?" he said.

I said "Yep" again.

School was pretty normal until the afternoon, when we had our class Valentine party! A bunch of us had brought goodies from home (Mirisen and I had brought some heart-shaped brownies we'd made), and Mrs. Banks let us set them out on the table in the back of the room. Then everyone put their Valentine boxes out on their desks, and we all got to go around and put our valentines in everyone's boxes.

When everyone had delivered all their valentines, we were allowed to get some snacks and go back to our seats to open our boxes. I got a cupcake, two cookies, one of my brownies, and some popcorn.

In my box, I found plenty of store-bought valentines, two homemade ones (one from Mirisen and the other from Rebecca, who's really artistic), lots of candy, and... at the very bottom of the box... a folded-up piece of white paper.

At first, I thought it was in there by mistake. But then I decided to unfold it, just to see if there was anything written on it. And... there was! It said:

"Dear Allisen,

I know I've been kind of annoying and you might not really like me that much. But I'm really sorry for annoying you and I want to be friends with you. I hope you forgive me.

Jack Bersner

P.S. do you want to go to the dance with me?"

I must have read that note about ten times before the meaning actually sunk in. Jack Bersner was apologizing and wanted to go to the dance with me? (And he had actually spelled my name right?) If he'd asked me a week ago I would have said NO WAY. But now... I don't know. I'm actually considering it.

February 15

Last night after our family Valentine's Day celebration, I asked my parents if I'd be allowed to go to the dance. They said that was fine. So today, I told Jack I'd go to the dance with him. I might regret it, but he hasn't really been annoying me anymore, so it should be okay.

I'm actually getting excited about this dance now that I have someone to go with. It seems like almost my entire class is going to be there. Even Mirisen's going, with her friend Domacie from last year's crazy school. Mirisen told me that Domacie went out shopping with his dad and bought a $200 tux to wear to the dance. Then she and I laughed our heads off. I mean, really, a $200 tux for a school dance? An <u>elementary</u> school dance? If you ask me, Domacie and his dad seem a little bit cuckoo in the head.

February 17

Two hours 'til the dance!!! I'm a little bit nervous. I've never been to a school dance before. I don't even know how to dance! I'm wearing my pretty red dress that I wear on Christmas and Valentine's Day. Mom's going to do my hair. Hopefully it will be fun...

February 18

The dance was a blast! There was loud music (but not <u>too</u> loud), and <u>lots</u> of refreshments. And we didn't even end up dancing much at all. Jack and I just hung out with a bunch of kids from our class and ate a ton of sweets. We danced in a huge circle with some of our classmates during one song, and for another a whole group of us participated in a "dancing contest" some kids from the other sixth grade class were holding. We were there for almost two hours, and it was a lot of fun! And, believe it or not, I had a <u>great</u> time hanging out with Jack! I mean, we're definitely not going to be best friends or anything like I'd originally hoped for the new student, but I'm glad I ended up going to the dance with him.

And do you know what I'm going to do now? Go sledding with my wonderful, non-broken, non-casted arm!

Book 7: Pupsurprise!

February 24

Hmmm. Something's going on here. I think Mom and Dad have a secret. I walked in on them discussing something in low voices this morning, and when they saw me they immediately stopped talking and started acting really suspicious, like, "Hi Allisen... how are you this morning?" and stuff like that. I wonder if the secret has to do with Harrisson's birthday six days from now. Are we going someplace special, maybe? I have no idea. But I'm going to solve this mystery!

February 27

More clues. Today Dad went up into the attic and started rummaging around for something. He started to bring something down but Mom said, "No! Not now! Wait until <u>after</u>..." and Dad was like, "Oh, yeah," and immediately brought whatever it was back into the attic. Mom then told me (because she saw me watching) that I wasn't allowed to go into the attic until after Harrisson's birthday. I never go in the attic anyway (except occasionally with Mom or Dad to get Christmas ornaments or something), but of course that made me <u>really</u> interested in what was up there. Now I know it most likely does have something to do with Harrisson's birthday... but why can't I see it? I wouldn't tell Harrisson what it is! I can keep a secret!

Well, at least I only have to wait three more days to find out.

March 1

Yay! Tomorrow is Harrisson's birthday, so I'll finally know what the secret is!!! (hopefully.) I haven't discovered any more clues.

March 2

Wow! Wowey-wow-WOW! Well, I know what the surprise was now! I'll start at the beginning.

So Mom picked me, Mirisen, Harrisson, and Pete up from school as usual. We went home and did normal stuff— homework, chores, free time —until dinner was ready. Dad got home at the exact time Mom finished cooking dinner (fried chicken, green beans, and box macaroni and cheese—Harrisson's request) and we all ate together. After we were all cleaned up from dinner, we ate Mom's delicious homemade chocolate cake and sang "Happy Birthday" and everything. Then Harrisson opened his presents. Then Dad left.

"Where's Daddy going?" Harrisson asked.

Mom smiled. "Well, we have one more birthday present for you... although this one's actually a present for the whole family."

"Is this the thing that was in the attic?" I asked.

Mom didn't answer. "Dad should be home in about ten minutes, so let's clean up all this wrapping paper and get the living room in order."

It was a long ten minutes. But finally, when I felt like I was about to burst with excitement, we heard the front door opening and Dad's voice yelling, "Surprise!"

Mirisen, Harrisson and I raced to the front door and saw Dad standing there with... A DOG!!!!!!!!!

We all ran to the dog, exclaiming stuff like, "Awwww!" The dog looked kind of like a beagle, but was a little bigger, with fur that was white, black, and kind of reddish-tan. Her ears were floppy but short, like Goldie's, and her tail was wagging at a million miles per hour.

"Whose dog is this?" I asked, hoping for a certain answer.

"It's ours," Dad said. That was just the answer I'd been hoping for.

"Yay! We have a dog! We have a dog!" Harrisson

started chanting.

"Is it a boy or a girl?" Mirisen asked. "And what's his or her name?"

"It's a girl," said Dad. "And I was thinking we'd all come up with a name together."

"Goldie!" exclaimed Harrisson immediately.

"We can't name her Goldie," I told him. "Goldie was our <u>other</u> dog. We can't name a dog the same name as a dog we already had." Harrisson was only four when Goldie died, so he remembers the name but I guess he doesn't remember Goldie much.

"How about Excitement?" Mirisen asked, watching the dog's excited body movements.

"No..." I said. "How about... Jackie?" I suggested that because the fur on her back was kind of the color of Jack Bersner's hair.

"How about Surprise, 'cause she was a surprise?" suggested Harrisson.

"I like that," said Mirisen.

"Yeah, me too," I said.

So it's settled. Our dog's name is Surprise!

March 3

Dad took all of Goldie's old things (her bed, her food dish, her leash, her toys) out of the attic last night (That was what Mom and Dad hadn't wanted us to see!) and we set them up for Surprise. Since she's already 10 months old and full-grown, we don't need to worry about potty-training her or anything. That's a relief!

We put her bed in Mirisen and Harrisson's room. I found this kind of unfair, but Mom reminded me that Sniffer sleeps on my bed nearly every night, so I guess it makes sense that I get to share a room with a pet and they get to share a room with a pet (and Pete doesn't care—he probably prefers sharing a room with no pet).

Speaking of our cats, Mom and Dad weren't sure how they'd react to Surprise. I mean, they were fine with Goldie, but Goldie was older and less energetic. Plus, they haven't been around a dog for two years, so it'll take some time to get used to. Dad said that the animal shelter people said that Surprise was good with other animals. I hope that's the case!

We introduced the cats to Surprise last night, sort of. I held Sniffer in my arms and let him and Surprise meet each other. Mom and Dad did the same with Leelee and Tuxio. All the cats seemed kind of wary, but Leelee was the only one who hissed.

Then, for the night, we shut Miri and Harry's door so Surprise wouldn't be able to get out. We <u>think</u> she'll be fine with the cats, but we want to supervise just in case.

Oh, and today, I told all my friends at school about Surprise. Rebecca asked to see pictures. Maybe I'll take some over the weekend with Mom's camera and see if I can get them printed so I can bring them in.

March 4

Yay! It's the weekend!! That means... time to play with Surprise!!!!!

March 6

Okay, I guess this having-a-puppy thing is hard work. Yesterday, I woke up to Harrisson crying because Surprise had chewed the ears off his favorite stuffed animal. Then later, Surprise saw Tuxio coming out from behind the couch, and started chasing after him. Tuxio just ran behind the couch, but Surprise was scratching up the wall and carpet and everything trying to get to him.

I'm starting to feel bad for our cats. Sniffer is now spending almost all of his time under my bed. Leelee spends almost all of her time hiding somewhere in Mom and Dad's room, usually where we can't find her. Tuxio is the only one who comes out, and Surprise chases him. I was worried about the cats when I went to school today. I don't think Surprise wants to hurt them—Mom says she probably just wants to play with them—but still. She's a lot bigger, so she could hurt them accidentally or something.

March 8

AAAAAAAAA!!!!!!!! We got home from school today and saw a disaster zone in the living room. There were candy wrappers and little bits of paper and even a tube of lipstick scattered across the carpet. And Mom's purse, with a couple bite marks in it, was lying right in the middle of the floor.

"Surprise!" Mom yelled sternly. We looked and saw Surprise sulking under the coffee table, trying to go unnoticed. She knew she'd done something wrong.

Mom shook her head. "This girl needs some exercise," she said, picking up the candy wrappers and such. "Why don't you four take her on a walk while I clean this up?"

"I'm outta here," said Pete, running upstairs.

Mom looked like she was about to yell after him, but I said quickly, "It's okay, the three of us can take her." I'd rather go on a walk without Pete anyway.

We attached her leash and grabbed a few plastic bags in case she pooped (I was hoping she wouldn't because I've never had to pick up poop before and I probably wouldn't even know how. Plus it's really gross). Then we walked outside.

"Can I hold her leash?" Harrisson asked.

I was not very smart. When Goldie was alive, we all used to take turns holding her leash, and it was okay, because Goldie was old and calm and mellow. So I thought it would be fine to let Harrisson hold Surprise's leash. I gave it to him as we walked down our super steep driveway.

We turned right and saw a lady walking a Dalmatian a little bit down the road. Surprise saw them too. She started running toward them. "Stop, stop, STOP!" Harrisson shouted, being pulled along with her. "Nooo!" The leash was ripped out of his hand and started dragging along the pavement.

My siblings and I all dashed after Surprise, but she was too fast for us. She reached the Dalmatian, who started growling slightly. The lady tried to pull her dog away, but that didn't do any good since Surprise wasn't on a leash.

I tackled Surprise and held onto her collar. She whined and struggled as the lady pulled her Dalmatian away and down the road some more. It took all three of us to keep a hold on Surprise.

"I think... I'll hold the leash from now on," I said.

"Let's just go back to the house," said Mirisen. "Mom or Dad can walk her later."

So that's what we did.

March 9

Dad's going to see if he can buy a fence to fence in our backyard. That way, Surprise can run around

100

freely without taking someone for an undesired sprint. In the meantime, Mom and Dad are going to walk her.

Mirisen got really upset today because she found two of her Barbies missing their arms. She also found one of Harrisson's Matchbox cars with teeth marks in it.

I've put all my Littlest Pet Shop things in a box that I keep on the top shelf of my closet. I'll only take them down when I want to play with them, and I'll make sure to clean everything up after. It's too bad, because I like keeping the little houses and stores set up around my room, and the toy pets each in their own little living area, but I am <u>not</u> taking any chances. I also now store all my stuffed animals <u>under</u> my comforter on my bed. It looks really lumpy, but Surprise hasn't noticed them yet. I would just keep my door shut, but Sniffer still likes to hide out in there (although he has gotten a <u>little</u> bit better, and will come out on his own for food and stuff).

<u>March 11</u>

I'm really worried. Last night, after I went to bed, I got up to go to the bathroom and heard Mom and Dad talking in low voices downstairs. I wasn't trying to eavesdrop or anything, but I caught snippets of their conversation anyway. "...so destructive..." "not really fair to the cats..." "stress..." "...have to take her back to the pound."

I felt chills go up my spine at those last words. Were they talking about Surprise? Taking her back to the <u>pound</u>? NOOOOOOOOOOO! Okay, so she is really destructive and chews up our toys and chases the cats and tears leashes out of people's hands. But she's OURS. You can't just adopt a dog and then give her <u>back</u>.

I'm not going to let that happen.

March 12

We can't leave food out on the table or counter anymore unless we push it waaaaay far back. I learned that the hard way. I made a ham and cheese sandwich for lunch, then turned around to put the ham and cheese back in the refrigerator, and when I went back to my sandwich it was gone. Surprise was sitting on the floor, gobbling it up.

We can <u>not</u> let stuff like this happen too often. If Surprise keeps damaging stuff and causing trouble, Mom and Dad will probably take her back.

When we got home from church today, I went all around the house cleaning things up and putting little things like toys and slippers and stuff away. Mom was looking at me really weirdly, because I usually hate cleaning up. I didn't tell her the <u>reason</u> I was cleaning.

Here's my line of thinking: if we always put everything away and don't leave things out where Surprise can get them, she won't wreck stuff. And if she doesn't wreck stuff, she's a perfect dog. And if she's a perfect dog, we'll get to keep her. So there.

March 13

I do not want to go to school today. I'm afraid that if I go to school, when I come back Surprise will be gone. Maybe I'll pretend I'm sick and see if Mom will let me stay home.

March 13, later

Mom made me go to school. I didn't pretend I was sick. I'm not that good of an actor, and besides, that's kind of like lying to your parents, which is something I <u>don't</u> do. But, on the ride to school, I did talk a lot about how excited I'd be to see Surprise and play with her when I got home.

I was still nervous the entire school day. When Mom picked us up, she didn't say anything one way or another. When we pulled in the driveway, I hopped out and ran inside the house. And... Surprise was there!!!! She jumped up and licked my face when I entered. I was so relieved to see her.

But I was not relieved to see one of Mom's magazines trashed around the upstairs hallway. Apparently, it had been on the floor of Mom and Dad's bedroom, and Surprise had decided it looked like a great chew toy. "Seriously, girl," I muttered to her, away from everyone else's hearing. "Do you want to stay with us or not? You have to stop making these messes!"

She just wagged her tail and looked at me.

March 15

Surprise is digging herself into a hole of trouble. I'm trying so hard to keep her out of trouble, but she keeps finding ways to mess things up. Today she had a good day... until Leelee sneaked out to the kitchen to get some food (by the way, we feed the cats on the counter now, instead of on the floor... you can imagine why!). Sniffer and Tuxio are pretty much fine now with Surprise (she chases them, but Sniffer's really fast and Tuxio just sits down like he doesn't care, which makes Surprise lose interest), but Leelee's been hiding in Mom and Dad's room since Harrisson's birthday. Anyway, Leelee was making her way toward the kitchen, and Surprise noticed her and bolted toward her. Leelee hissed and started running. Surprise chased her all around the kitchen and knocked over a chair. Leelee ran into the open pantry and Surprise chased her in there. Leelee then started attacking Surprise's face. Mom and I were in the kitchen, and we both ran over and tried to pry them away from each other. When we finally did, Surprise's face had a bunch of scratches from Leelee's claws. "Well, you deserve it," Mom said admonishingly.

Leelee was okay, but in a bad mood and really

freaked out. She kept hissing and the hair on her back kept arching and her tail was about ten times bigger than normal. I picked her up to bring her to Mom and Dad's room, and she hissed at me.

I'm still worried every day that when I get home from school, Surprise won't be there. I have no idea how to get her to behave.

March 16

Waaaaaaaaaaaahaaaaaaaaaaahaaaaaaaaaaaaa.
Dad just gave us the news at dinner tonight.

"Just as a heads-up, I need to tell you guys something," he said. He sounded serious. "I'm sure everyone's noticed the messes Surprise has been getting into..." he continued.

"Yeah, she chewed up one of my road pieces!" exclaimed Harrisson indignantly. "And three of our stuffed animals! And some of Miri's dolls and things too!"

"Yeah, and I think she might have eaten some of our Legos, because I can't find them anywhere," added Mirisen.

"Exactly," said Dad. "She's quite a handful, and Mom and I are pretty stressed out having to deal with her all the time. When I saw her at the animal shelter, I picked her out because she was really cute and I liked her personality. And she does seem to be good with people. But I didn't expect her to be so destructive."

"She's not <u>that</u> destructive," I piped up, because I knew what was coming. Mirisen and Harrisson looked at me like I was crazy.

"She chewed the leg off of your tiger," Harrisson reminded me.

"Only because it was in your room and you left it on the floor," I shot back. "If we keep everything cleaned up and out of sight, she won't chew it up."

"That's true," said Dad. "But she terrorizes the cats, and when I take her for walks, she chases anything that moves, and she has a way of getting into <u>everything</u>, even things we think are safe. For instance, when I came down for breakfast this morning, she had torn open a box of cereal and left it scattered everywhere around the floor."

"So we just need to train her," I said.

"Well..." said Dad. "We can try. I try, during our walks. But what I wanted to tell you guys is—and I know you're not going to like this—if this keeps up, we're going to have to bring Surprise back to the animal shelter. We can see about getting a different dog— maybe an older one who won't be so much trouble. But we can't have a dog who's this destructive."

So there it was. Out in the open. They <u>did</u> want to bring her back.

Of course, my siblings felt like I did.

"What?" exclaimed Mirisen. "You can't bring her

back! She's ours! You signed adoption papers and everything!"

"Noooooo!" cried Harrisson. "She's my birthday present! She's special! We can't get a different dog!"

"Yeah, how would you feel if when you were a kid, your parents said you were too much trouble so they had to get rid of you?" added Mirisen.

That was a really good comparison so I said, "Yeah, and got another kid in your place? One who was older and not as destructive."

Dad put his hand up. "Hey, listen, I didn't say we will definitely be doing that. I just said if it keeps up like this, that's what we'll have to do. I'd like to find a way to make it work without bringing her back, but I just don't know what else we can do."

"We'll figure something out," I said. "Right, guys?"

Mirisen and Harrisson both nodded. "Definitely," said Mirisen.

"We'll give it a week," said Dad. "If there's been a decent amount of improvement in one week, or if a solution has been found, we won't give her back. But if not, it may be our only option."

It will never be our only option. Now we just need to think of a solution.

March 18

Ugh, this is so frustrating! I can't think of any

ideas!! Harrisson, Mirisen and I have started having "brain-storming sessions" every night. Mirisen suggested an obedience school, but when we said that to Mom and Dad, they said it would cost too much and obedience schools don't really address problems like chewing and chasing anyway. Harrisson suggested that we put Surprise in time-out or take away dessert when she does something bad, but I pointed out that time-outs only work if the person being punished understands <u>why</u> they're in time-out. And the dessert idea was just silly, because Surprise doesn't get dessert, and, even if she did, she wouldn't make the connection.

March 20

I called Emalie Maye today to see if she could come up with any ideas. She suggested obedience school. Nope. I was going to ask the kids who I sit with at lunch if they had any ideas, but everyone was talking about other stuff and I didn't get a chance to say anything.

ONLY THREE DAYS LEFT.

March 21

Yay! I think I might have found a solution! During computer class today, I went on the Internet and was trying to look up ideas for how to train dogs not to chew stuff. Jack Bersner was sitting next to me, and he looked over onto the screen.

"Do you have a dog who chews stuff?" he asked.

"Yeah," I said. "She chews up everything, and she chases our cats, and she steals food off counters, and my dad said that if we can't find a way to make her stop doing that by the 23rd, we'll have to take her back to the pound."

"Could you get her a training collar?" asked Jack.

"What's that?"

"There are a couple different types. Some of them have zappers and others have smells and others have like really high-pitched noises. There's a remote that goes to the collar, and when the dog does something they're not supposed to, you hit the button on the remote and it zaps them or puts off a smell they don't like or makes a sound that's so high-pitched only dogs can hear it. We have a zap one for my dog, but I know people who have the other kinds too."

I thought about it. That sounded like a pretty smart idea. If Surprise kept having the same thing happen to her each time she did something she wasn't supposed to, maybe she'd learn. But— "What do you mean by <u>zap</u>?" I asked. "That sounds like it would hurt."

He shrugged. "I zapped myself once to find out what it felt like. It doesn't exactly <u>hurt</u>. It just feels really weird. And, I mean, maybe it hurts a little, but that's kind of the point. It's not like torture, it's just like

'Oh, I'd better not do that again.' You know?"

I think a training collar is a <u>great</u> idea. I suggested it to Mom and she said, "Hmm, maybe we could try it." Now I'm just waiting for Dad to get home so I can suggest it to him as well!

March 21, later

Yes! Dad said we could get a training collar for Surprise!!!! He said, "It's worth a try." Now we just need to decide what kind we're getting. I'm personally not too sure about the zapping one—I know Jack said it wasn't too bad, but I still don't like the concept that much—but we know we can't get the noise one because the cats would be able to hear it too. My parents said the smell one might be the same way. So we're probably getting a zap collar. But oh well—I'm just thrilled that we'll get to keep Surprise!!! Well, if it works.

I'm praying it'll work.

March 22

Dad bought a zap collar and we tried it out on Surprise today. Here's what we do: whenever Surprise starts doing something she shouldn't—such as chewing something other than a chew toy, chasing one of the cats, taking something off the counter or table, or chasing something on a walk—we say, "Surprise, NO!" in a very stern voice. If she doesn't listen, we press the little button on the remote, and it sends a shock to her collar.

When we first put the collar on Surprise, she didn't do anything. She probably knew she was being watched. But later, we caught her chewing on Mirisen's sneaker, and Dad said "Surprise, NO!" When Surprise didn't listen, Dad zapped her. She kind of jumped a little, like, "What was that?" and then went back to the shoe. But when Dad did the same thing again, I think she got the message.

Dad said we have to be patient. We can't expect the collar to work right away. But—good news!—he's not bringing her back to the pound tomorrow!

March 26

We've had Surprise's zap collar for four days now, and she's responding well to it. She's stopped chasing the cats (although here's the funny part—she and Tuxio sometimes seem to <u>play</u> together!) and she's getting better about not chewing stuff or stealing food when we're around. Dad says she's better on walks too, although he's still going to put up a fence around our backyard so she has more space to run.

She still isn't great about behaving when we're <u>not</u> around, but we'll work on that. Maybe put up surveillance cameras with our voices programmed into them or something, who knows? For now, what I'm glad about is that Surprise is making progress, and that we <u>don't</u> have to give her back to the pound. Thanks to Jack and his wonderful idea. I've been keeping him posted about how Surprise is doing. Maybe he can come over and meet her sometime!

Okay, I have to stop writing now, because I'm going to go play with Surprise and her favorite <u>real</u> chew toy!

Book 8: Going To Carolina

April 1

Wow, what a great day. First we went to a McDonald's in Antarctica, and then we visited the Museum of Deserted Bodies, where ghosts float around. For dinner, we ate broiled beds and mashed ovens, and we fell asleep on the ceiling (since we had eaten all our beds). It was awesome!

...APRIL FOOL!!!

I know, I know. It's a silly April fool's joke that you probably didn't believe and thought was really crazy. But the joke Mom and Dad played on us this morning was a lot more realistic! Dad came into my room all urgent and shook me, saying, "Allisen! Get up! It's seven-thirty! You're gonna be late for school!"

I bolted upright, jumped out of bed, and started rummaging around for clothes. I had actually already gotten dressed and started downstairs for breakfast by the time I realized, "Wait a minute... isn't it Saturday?!?"

Mom and Dad were laughing. Apparently, Mom had done the same thing to Mirisen and Harrisson. Mirisen had reacted like I had, but then Harrisson had just said, "It's Saturday," and they'd gone back to sleep.

I was kind of mad at first, but then Mom and Dad said I could go back to sleep and once I woke up they'd even make French toast for breakfast to make up for it. (And that was <u>not</u> an April Fool's joke!)

April 3

Yes! Best news ever! For Easter vacation this year, we get to go to Carolina's house!!!!!!!! Yippee!!!!!!!!!

Carolina's my favorite cousin. She's Mirisen's and Harrisson's favorite cousin too, and she's also Mirisen's best friend. We have three other cousins, who live in California (Carolina's family lives in Pennsylvania), but we don't see them much. We usually get together with Carolina's family a couple times a year.

Easter vacation starts on April 13 this year (that's the Thursday before Easter) and goes all the way until the 23rd. We're going to leave on the 12th right after school gets out, and stay until probably the 22nd. And here's the great part: Carolina goes to a Fun House school like we do, so she has the same vacation!!!!!!! We won't have to worry about her being in school and us having nothing to do! And Carolina's birthday is on April 17th, so we'll be there for that too!

I'm so excited. I don't know how I'm going to wait for ten whole days!

April 6

Six more days!

April 10

We started packing today. Since we're going to be there during Easter, I packed my special Easter dress and my fancy shoes. I also packed a bunch of normal clothes, plus some books to read in the car, and I'm going to bring some of my stuffed animals and this journal too. Mirisen loaded up practically her entire suitcase with Barbies and Barbie accessories, and had to store some of her clothes in Harrisson's suitcase. But that's because Barbies are Mirisen and Carolina's special thing. I play Barbies with Mirisen sometimes, but more often we play with Pound Puppies or Littlest Pet Shops or stuffed animals (because those are the things I like better, and Mirisen likes them too). But Carolina is practically obsessed with Barbies, so she and Miri always have fun playing with them together.

Two days left!

April 11

We're leaving tomorrow! We just finished loading up the van after dinner tonight. Mom and Dad are going to pick us up from school tomorrow and we're going to drive straight on to Carolina's house from there. It's about a seven hour drive (taking into account stopping to use the bathroom and stuff), so we should get there around ten at night. I'd rather get there earlier in the evening so we still have time to <u>do</u> stuff and not just go straight to bed, but oh well. Mom and Dad sometimes let us stay up late if it's not a school night and we're doing something fun.

April 12

And we're off! It's 3:38 right now and we've been driving for about half an hour. I'm sitting in one of the middle-row seats, and Pete's in the other one (but it's okay, because he has headphones on and is staring out the window. He's mad because he didn't want to come along but Mom and Dad made him). Mirisen and Harrisson are in their booster seats in the back, and Surprise is right now sitting in the middle seat between them. Sniffer's cat carrier is right in front of my feet, and every so often I reach in and pet him. Leelee's carrier is between Mom and Dad, and Tuxio, who never travels in a carrier, is I think under the backseat. Oooh! I just realized! Aunt Brenda, Uncle Joe, and Carolina have never met Surprise! I bet they'll love her.

April 12, later

We're here! But Carolina isn't. Aunt Brenda told us she's sleeping over at her new friend Avy's house tonight. "They had it planned a long time ago," she said apologetically. "Before we knew you guys were coming. But she'll be back in the morning, and you'll see her then!"

Since Carolina isn't here, there's really no point in Mirisen, Harrisson and me staying up any later, so we're just going to go to bed as soon as Aunt Brenda finishes blowing up the air mattresses. Mirisen, Harrisson and I are all sleeping in Carolina's room, as usual. Harrisson and I will share a queen-sized air mattress, and Mirisen will share Carolina's bed (although for tonight, I guess she'll have it all to herself!). Mom, Dad, and Pete get the guest room.

Aunt Brenda and Uncle Joe were excited to meet Surprise. And my siblings and I were excited to meet Mitzy, Carolina's new gerbil! We didn't even know she had gotten a gerbil, but apparently Carolina just got her a week ago from a friend at school. She is fluffy and brown and very soft.

Well, Mom just came in and told me to brush my teeth, so I guess I'll go do that. I'll write more tomorrow!

April 13

Well, Carolina's here now. And she's... well, <u>different</u>.

We were all up already before she came back this morning. Aunt Brenda made waffles, and we were all sitting around eating them when the front door opened and we heard, "We're here!"

Carolina then came into sight. The first thing I noticed was that she'd gotten a haircut since I'd last seen her in November—her hair now only comes down to her chin in sort of a bob style. Then I noticed she was wearing dangly earrings, lipstick, and what looked like a little bit of eye makeup. She's only eight! Even <u>I</u> don't have pierced ears or wear makeup yet!

Aunt Brenda noticed the makeup and frowned. "Is that makeup, honey?" she asked.

Carolina waved her hand in the air. "Yeah, Desiree let us use it and we played Beauty Shop. It's fine." She then seemed to notice my family sitting around her kitchen table. She shrieked excitedly and ran over to Mirisen. "Miri! You're here! Oh my gosh, Miri, you've got to meet Avy! Come on!" She grabbed Mirisen's hand and dragged her over to the entrance where she'd originally appeared.

It was then that I noticed another girl standing there. She had glossy blond hair cut in the exact same style as Carolina's, and was wearing a bunch of really obvious makeup. Her clothes were the type I might expect from a high-schooler, and as she tucked a strand of hair behind her ear, I noticed that her ears were <u>double</u> pierced.

"Avy, meet Mirisen. Mirisen, meet Avy," said Carolina. "Avy is my best friend in the entire world. She moved into the house right across the street a couple months ago, and now we're BFFs. And Mirisen is my cousin from New Hampshire."

I noticed Mirisen looked a little upset at this introduction.

"Hey, Mom, can me and Avy go back over to Avy's house? And can Miri come with us? I wanna show her something."

Aunt Brenda looked over at Mom and Dad, who shrugged. "I guess that's okay, if Mirisen wants to do that," said Aunt Brenda.

"Yay!" Carolina didn't ask Mirisen if she wanted to come. She just put one arm around Mirisen and the other around Avy and said, "Let's go!"

It's been a few hours and they haven't come back yet. Harrisson and I ran around in the backyard with Surprise for a while, and then went out front to see if we could see the girls. We couldn't, so we went back inside and tried to find something to do. Now Harrisson's watching Mitzy (who's <u>sleeping</u>) and I'm writing.

This is boring.

April 14

Mirisen and Carolina finally came back last night, around dinnertime. Carolina spent the entire dinnertime chatting on and on about Avy and her other two friends, Jessie and Marna, who she apparently met at some after-school theater camp she and Avy went to in February. "So now the four of us are best friends," she said. "But me and Avy are still <u>best</u> best friends, of course. But the four of us have, like, a club? And Avy's the president. And I'm the vice president. And then Jessie and Marna are, like, secretaries or something." She looked at Aunt Brenda. "Oh, I forgot to ask you. Can Jessie and Marna come over tomorrow? Pleeease?"

"Honey, your cousins from New Hampshire are here. Don't you think you should be spending some time with them?"

"Well... Mirisen's going to hang out with us, and... come <u>on</u>, Mom, it's school vacation! Avy and Jessie and Marna only have tomorrow and the weekend and Monday left before they have to go back to school!"

Well, Jessie and Marna didn't come over today. But Avy did. She and Carolina went out front, and Mirisen, Harrisson and I followed.

"So what do you guys want to play?" asked Harrisson. "Tag?"

"Carolina and I are going to be doing gymnastics," said Avy.

Mirisen's face fell. She's terrible at gymnastics. "Can we do something... different?" she asked.

"Yes," said Avy. "You can. But Carolina and I are doing gymnastics." She then did a perfect cartwheel.

"I can't do those," said Harrisson.

"Well, maybe we can do something else in a little bit, but right now we're doing gymnastics," said Carolina. "If you want, you can be the judge."

Harrisson was the judge for like two minutes before he got bored. I started doing gymnastics with Carolina and Avy—I'm not great but I can do okay cartwheels and stuff like that—but I stopped when I saw that Mirisen was sitting on the front step, looking like she was about to cry.

I went over to her. "Do you wanna go do something else?" I asked her.

She shrugged. "I want to hang out with Carolina. But she's too busy doing things with Aaaay-vee." She said Avy's name almost sarcastically.

"Well..." I wasn't sure what to do. "At least we'll have time to spend with her tonight, after Avy goes home. Right now, how about you and I go play Barbies together?" It wasn't what I really wanted to do, but I wanted to cheer her up.

"Okay," said Mirisen glumly. "Maybe we can make

a cool set-up for Carolina and me to play with later."

April 15

Ugh. I can't believe tomorrow's Easter. It sure doesn't feel like it.

Mirisen and I played Barbies yesterday and set up all of the dolls so that Mirisen and Carolina could play with them later. But Carolina didn't come back from Avy's house until dinnertime <u>again</u>, and after dinner we went to a Good Friday service at Carolina's church, and by the time we got home it was time for bed.

Then, this morning, Avy came over bright and early, while we were still eating the donuts Uncle Joe brought home for breakfast. "You wanna hang out after you're done eating?" she asked Carolina.

"Sure!" said Carolina.

"Carolina," said Aunt Brenda. "It would be nice if you could find something to do with your cousins as well. They're not going to be here forever."

After breakfast, I went to the bathroom to brush my teeth, and when I came out, I saw Carolina, Mirisen, and Avy heading into Carolina's room.

"So, what do you guys wanna do?" asked Carolina.

"How about we play Barbies?" Mirisen suggested. "Allisen and I set these up last night, and—"

Avy cut her off. "Barbies are for babies. We're too old for dolls."

I peeked in. I saw Mirisen looking at Carolina for help. "We're not too old for dolls," she said. "Carolina and I play Barbies all the time. Right, Carolina?"

I saw Carolina scrunch her face. "Well... we <u>used</u> to, when we were younger. But... I mean... we <u>are</u> getting kind of old for dolls, I guess..."

"Carolina, you're <u>eight</u>!" protested Mirisen.

"Nine in two days," Carolina shot back.

"So what? Allisen's eleven and she still plays with dolls! It doesn't matter how old you are!"

"Um, it kinda does," said Avy in a snobby voice. "You don't want people thinking you're a <u>baby</u>, do you?"

Mirisen looked herself over. "Hmm, let's see. I have an advanced vocabulary... I read books at an eighth-grade reading level... I have long hair... I'm almost four feet tall... I have permanent teeth... I don't think I could be mistaken for a baby no matter <u>what</u> I'm doing."

"Guys!" said Carolina. "Stop it. Mirisen, if you don't want to hang out with us, just go away and leave us alone."

I saw the hurt on Mirisen's face. I saw the triumphant expression on Avy's. I was about to step in and say something when Mirisen stood up and said, "You know what? I have better ways to spend my time than being treated like dirt by people like you. Have fun doing nothing."

She kept her control as she walked out of the room and past me. Avy shut the door behind her. I followed Mirisen in to the guest room, where she laid down on Mom and Dad's air mattress and started crying.

Carolina <u>used</u> to be my favorite cousin. Now she's a jerk.

April 16

Happy Easter!

We dyed Easter eggs last night, and it sort of seemed to patch things up between Mirisen and Carolina a little. I mean, Carolina acted like nothing had ever happened, and complimented Mirisen on her egg designs and stuff. Mirisen was a little less-than-friendly toward Carolina, but not too much. I guess maybe she was glad <u>she</u> was with Carolina and Avy wasn't.

We went to church today, and it was actually an Avy-free zone. Whoopee. When we got home, the four of us kids got Easter baskets, and then we had an Easter egg hunt. I sort of expected Carolina to say something like, "I'm too old for Easter egg hunts," but she didn't. Instead, she seemed to have a lot of fun running around looking for eggs. I think Mirisen had fun too, but I could tell she was still thinking about yesterday.

We had a nice large dinner, and by the time dinner was over, Carolina was blabbering Mirisen's ears off. She kept talking about the birthday party she's having tomorrow. "It's gonna be so great! Jessie and Marna are coming over, and Avy of course, and we'll probably have a club meeting while they're here, and it'll be so much fun! I can't wait! I haven't seen them in forever!"

Later, when we were getting ready for bed, Mirisen came over to me. "If Jessie and Marna are anything like Avy, this is going to be the worst party I have ever attended," she told me.

"Well, keep your hopes up," I said. "Maybe they're entirely different."

We can hope.

April 18

WHEN will this vacation be OVER?!?!?!?!? I'm so sick and tired of it!

So Carolina's birthday party was yesterday. She was super excited and running all around the house before it started. She grabbed Mirisen's hands and started dancing around, and then Harrisson joined in and they all danced in a little circle. Mirisen was even smiling a little.

But around 1:00, Carolina's friends started showing up. Avy came first, of course. She and Mirisen ignored each other. Then Marna arrived, and then Jessie. Marna had bright red hair and giggled at everything Jessie, Avy, or Carolina said. Jessie had black hair with a blue streak in it, and was very dramatic about everything. They both had pierced ears.

"Club meeting!" declared Avy. "We'll do it in Carolina's room." She led Carolina, Jessie, and Marna over to Carolina's room, and Mirisen hung back awkwardly.

"Carolina, aren't you going to invite Mirisen?" asked Aunt Brenda.

"Oh," said Carolina. "Sure, Miri, you can come."

Avy rolled her eyes and whispered something to Jessie and Marna, who giggled. Mirisen glared at them out of the corner of her eye, but followed the group.

They shut the door behind them, and I stood at the door to listen in. Harrisson came over to see what I was doing, and I put a finger to my lips and pointed at the closed door. He understood.

I couldn't hear much at first. Then I heard my sister's voice, because she was shouting: "Just because you have four holes in your earlobes and your big sister lets you use her makeup does <u>not</u> make you any more mature than the rest of us! In fact, you're <u>im</u>mature, because you think things like that make you a big shot!"

"Well, you're not even part of our club," I heard Avy's voice shoot back. "So just stop pretending to be part of a group. You're never going to have any friends. Guys, you know what this girl does for fun? <u>Homework</u>."

I heard giggles. Then Mirisen's voice, the voice

she uses when she's trying to stop tears from coming out. "I came here to spend time with my cousin. Not to have her taken away by a bunch of silly, crazy, pathetic wannabes who—"

"Don't talk like that about my friends!" Carolina interjected angrily. "Don't you <u>dare</u>! These are—"

"But I came here to spend time with you! You can't spend every second with these people and treat me like I'm a rotten egg!"

"You're <u>acting</u> like a rotten egg!"

"Well, you know what? I don't even want to hang out with all you monsters. I'm leaving!"

I jumped back, pulling Harrisson with me. Mirisen whipped the door open and stomped past us. Harrisson stared after her, wide-eyed. I didn't know whether to try to distract him or go after Mirisen or go in and yell at Carolina and all her mean friends.

This is without a doubt the worst vacation ever.

<u>April 19</u>

It's been two days since Carolina's birthday disaster. She and Mirisen aren't speaking to one another. Mirisen has even moved into the guest room with Mom and Dad and Pete. Harrisson and I are still sleeping in Carolina's room, but it's not very fun. There's no whispering and giggling at night, no staying up late and playing games like we usually do when we're here. So nighttime stinks.

Daytime could maybe be tolerable if Carolina was still spending the entire day over at Avy's house. But Avy's back in school now (she goes to a public school), so it's just me and Harrisson and sullen Mirisen and bratty Carolina stuck at home together. Mirisen usually reads and Carolina usually plays on the computer and changes her clothes a million times and who knows what else. Harrisson's asked us all to play stuff like Tag and Capture the Flag with him, but Mirisen and Carolina don't want to play anything if the other is playing. I've played Matchbox cars and stuffed animals with him a couple times, mainly just because I felt sorry for him having nothing to do. But it wasn't that fun. When you're at your cousin's house, you're supposed to be playing with <u>your cousin</u>, not just your little brother who you get to play with all the time at home.

I called Carolina out today. "You're being a total brat," I told her. "Mirisen just wants to spend time with you—"

"No, <u>she's</u> being selfish," Carolina argued. "I can have friends if I want, and if she doesn't like them, that's her problem."

Avy came over after school today. I tried talking to her too. "Just because you and Mirisen have different interests doesn't give you the right to be mean to her," I told her.

She just rolled her eyes. "I'm never mean to people unless they're mean to me first. First time she came over to my house she said my shirt was too 'old' for me and kept talking about how she wanted Carolina and her to leave."

Aunt Brenda thinks Avy and Mirisen are jealous of each other, because they both want Carolina's attention. She tried to tell Carolina that, but Carolina was still too mad at Mirisen to care.

I'm counting down the days till we go home.

April 20

Oh, no. This is bad. Carolina's gerbil, Mitzy, is extremely sick. She hasn't moved all day. She's just lying in her cage as a lump. Carolina has been crying for hours. One teeny little mean part of me almost thinks it serves her right for being so mean to Mirisen. But I also feel really really sorry for her. Maybe I'll go in in a little while to see if there's anything I can do to help.

April 20, later

I did go in to comfort Carolina. Harrisson did too, and, to my huge surprise, so did Mirisen. Mirisen sat on the bed next to her and Harrisson and I sat on the floor.

"Hey Carolina..." said Mirisen. "I'm sorry for insulting your friends. And I hope Mitzy will be okay."

I heard the doorbell ring, and a few moments later, Avy came in, looking truly concerned. She didn't even seem bothered by the fact that my siblings and I were there. She sat down on the other side of Carolina and put an arm around her. "How's Mitzy doing?" she asked worriedly.

"Not good," sobbed Carolina.

Mirisen gently opened the top of the cage and peered in. Mitzy was lying on her side, breathing heavily. After a few moments of studying her, Mirisen put the cover of the cage back on. "Carolina?" she said.

Carolina raised her head and looked at her.

"I'm not entirely sure about this, but I think Mitzy's pregnant."

"P-pregnant? But...how..."

"See how her belly's kind of puffy? That's how gerbils look when they're pregnant," Mirisen said. "And she's lying on her side, which suggests she's about to go into labor."

Avy gave Mirisen an almost admiring look. "How do you know all that?" she asked.

"I'm interested in this kind of stuff," Mirisen responded.

"Well..." said Avy. "That's kinda cool."

Avy stayed a while longer and asked Carolina if she wanted to have a fashion show. "And...you could be in it too," she said hesitantly to Mirisen. "If you want to be."

Mirisen gave her a tentative smile. "Okay."

"A fashion show?" complained Harrisson. "That's boring."

"We can all do something together later," Carolina promised him. "But I want to stay in here right now to keep an eye on Mitzy. I'll do the fashion show."

I think things are going to be all right with Mirisen and Avy!

April 22

We're driving home now. Our last two days at Carolina's house were awesome! Let's see. Harrisson and I had just started trying to decide what to do (after I finished writing that last entry) when we heard shrieks coming from Carolina's room. We ran in and saw Carolina, Mirisen, and Avy all huddled excitedly around Mitzy's cage. The adults came in too, and we all watched as Mitzy gave birth to five tiny, hairless gerbil babies! Uncle Joe and Aunt Brenda were shocked. They hadn't known she was pregnant.

Uncle Joe went on the computer and looked up how to take care of gerbil babies. Aunt Brenda told Carolina she wouldn't be able to keep all of them, so Carolina asked Mirisen and Avy if they wanted any. They both did, of course. And guess what—Uncle Joe found out that gerbils do best living with other gerbils, so Mom and Dad are letting us get TWO! We'll have to make sure they're either both boys or both girls, though, because we don't want to end up with a bunch of gerbil babies!

Yesterday and today my siblings and I spent time with Carolina. We played a spy game and then played Capture the Flag outside. Then Mirisen and Carolina played Barbies, and Harrisson and I joined them. Harrisson stuffed his Barbie family in a car and had them do really crazy things. When Avy came over after school, she and Mirisen and Carolina all hung out together and did not fight!!!! Mirisen and Carolina even managed to persuade Avy to participate in a Barbie fashion show.

Today we left for home around 3:00. We'll arrive late again, but at least we don't have school tomorrow! Last night, Mirisen, Carolina, Harrisson and I stayed up really late giggling and talking (we're all sleeping in Carolina's room again) and then today before we left we played the spy game together again.

In a couple months, Carolina and her parents are going to come visit us and bring our new gerbils. I can't wait! And I'm sure that this time, we'll have as much fun for the entire visit as we had the last two days of this one.

Book 9: Showtime Star

April 28

Ooooh! Exciting news! Today Mrs. Banks announced that our sixth-grade class, along with the other sixth-grade class, is going to be putting on a class play! The play we'll be doing is <u>Turkeys Lurking</u>—actually a musical— which is about a bunch of turkeys who escape from a farm around Thanksgiving time and a girl who keeps seeing them everywhere (but no one believes her). Some of the kids in my class think <u>Turkeys Lurking</u> is babyish, but I like it! Mrs. Banks passed out scripts before we went home for the weekend, and I read the entire thing almost immediately.

Auditions are on Monday, May 1st. Mrs. Banks told us to read and study the scripts over the weekend, so we'll know what parts we want to audition for and be ready for them. We don't have to have anything memorized for Monday, but we should still be ready to read with expression for the part we want.

I think I know what part I want. I want to be Maria, the main character. Maria has the most lines and a bunch of solo singing parts. Plus she has my mom's name, which is an added bonus! Mirisen's going to try out for Katie, Maria's know-it-all older sister. She'd be absolutely <u>perfect</u> for that part, because she really is a know-it-all sometimes. And the fact that she's nine and in sixth grade makes it obvious that she's smart. Plus, if I get the part of Maria and Mirisen gets the part of Katie, we'll be acting out sisters, and we really are sisters! So it'll be perfect.

I can't wait for auditions.

May 1

Auditions are today!!!!!! I'm soooooooo nervous. I hope I do well. I hope I get the part of Maria. Mirisen and I rehearsed a bunch of lines together over the weekend. We went over pretty much all the parts of the script that have Maria and Katie talking to each other. Mirisen even started memorizing some of the Katie lines already—she's really good at memorizing stuff. Plus she's great at both acting and singing. I'm just an okay actress and a mediocre singer. Plus I don't have anything memorized. That's okay, right?

May 1, later

Auditions are over! We went in alphabetical order by last names, so Mirisen was last, and I was second-last. That's what I hate about alphabetical order. With a name like Allisen Zepetto, I'm always either one of the first or one of the last, whether they go by first names or last names or even backward.

Nicholas Alldren was first. He tried out for the part of Maria's dad, and he was okay. Then a kid named Ryan Baker from the other class tried out for John, Maria's older brother, and was pretty good. Then Jack Bersner tried out for a turkey, which made everyone laugh, especially when he pretended to peck Mrs. Banks on the arm.

Sara Corey was next, trying out for Sarah in the play, Maria's best friend. She was pretty good. I hoped she'd get the part because she and I are friends in real life, so it wouldn't be hard to act like best friends in the play.

The auditions took kind of a long time.. Everyone had to sing a small piece of a song—it didn't have to be one from the play because our teachers hadn't given us a rehearsal CD—and read a few lines of the part we wanted, with Mrs. Banks or Mrs. Thera (the other sixth-grade teacher) being the other characters. Not every-one tried out for a part—Natalia Frink, Austin Kline, Michael Savisky, and some kids from Mrs. Thera's class said that acting wasn't their thing or that they would be too nervous to perform in front of people, and Rebecca Hanson and a couple others wanted to do the scenery rather than act. But twenty-six kids went before me, including Nick, Jack, Ryan and Sara. Some were good, some were not-so-good, and some were in the middle. Seven girls auditioned for Maria. Two weren't that good, but four were all right, and one of them—Ashellie Tager from Mrs. Thera's class—was awesome. I have some competition!

Finally, finally, FINALLY it was my turn. I sang part of the song "Goodbye Yellow Brick Road" by Elton John, and tried to be very emphatic with my lines. "I am not kidding, Sarah. I saw a turkey! A turkey, right here in the school!"

Mrs. Banks said Sarah's line, "But how would a turkey get into the school?"

I shrugged dramatically. "I have no idea. I mean, it's not like all the windows are open or anything. But I'm absolutely certain that it was a turkey I saw." I added a few words, but that was okay. Or at least, it would have been okay if Mirisen hadn't been right behind me.

Mirisen was absolutely flawless. She's born to perform. Of course, it helped that the way Katie acts is kind of how Mirisen acts in real life anyway (Well, how Mirisen acts when she's annoyed, at least).

"Excuse me, I couldn't help overhearing your conversation. John, is it possible that your intention was to say the word 'hallucinations?'" Yep, that's Mirisen all right.

For some odd reason, I thought I saw Mrs. Banks frowning a little as Mirisen said her lines. When Mirisen finished, Mrs. Banks spoke. "Mirisen... you were fabulous, I'll give you that. But is there any other part you might want to audition for? It's just that... well, Katie is Maria's <u>older</u> sister, and you're... well, younger than the rest of the class..."

I felt immediately angry at that comment. So what if Mirisen's younger than the rest of us? It just means she's smart. And isn't that kind of like discrimination, saying she can't have a certain part just because of her age?

Mirisen just shrugged. "Katie would be my first choice, but I'd be content with any role."

Mrs. Banks nodded. "Well, this wraps up our auditions, boys and girls. I'll look over my notes tonight, and tomorrow you'll find out what part you got. I'll also try to have the rehearsal CDs for everyone tomorrow."

Maria, Maria, Maria, pleeeeeeeease let me get Maria!

May 2

GRRRRRRR! Guess who got my part? Yep, that's

right, my little sister. Mirisen is Maria.

Here are some other names and their parts: Nick Alldren: Father. Elizabeth Johnson: Mother. Sara Corey: Sarah. Jack Bersner: turkey. Keegan Jones: John (Maria's brother). Ashellie Tager: Mrs. Brett (Maria's teacher). And do you know who I am? KATIE! It's kind of funny how I wanted to be Maria and got the part of Katie, and Mirisen wanted to be Katie and got the part of Maria. Oh well. At least I didn't get the part of a turkey or one of Maria's random classmates, because they have hardly any lines at all. In the scope of the play, Katie is actually a fairly small part, but at least she has lines throughout the entire play, and a small singing role. And at least I'll know how to talk like her, with a sister like Mirisen!

The play is going to be on Friday, May 26th. We're actually performing it twice—once during the school day for the kindergarten through fifth graders, and once at night for all our parents and everyone. That means we have less than a month to practice! Yikes! Mrs. Banks said we're going to start by taking about thirty minutes at the end of each school day to rehearse with Mrs. Thera's class, and then we'll start having longer rehearsals once we get closer to the actual event.

May 3

First rehearsal today! We just read straight

through the script, everyone getting used to their parts and everything. We skipped all the songs, even though we all have our rehearsal CDs now. I'm glad we skipped the songs, because I wouldn't have felt comfortable singing my part yet. I don't know all the lyrics.

May 5

Yikes! Mrs. Banks and Mrs. Thera said that we should all try to have our lines memorized by Monday! I'm not even close to that. I have like three of my twenty-eight lines memorized. And the singing part— forget it! Usually it's pretty easy for me to memorize stuff set to music, but my particular solo is supposed to be sung really fast, and to top it all off, it's a tongue twister! I've never been good at tongue twisters. I kind of feel like Mrs. Banks and Mrs. Thera are asking too much of us—I mean, we have to <u>perform</u> in just three weeks! That's only 15 days of rehearsal, because we don't practice on weekends!

May 8

Today's rehearsal was a disaster. A complete and utter failure. <u>Nobody</u> has their lines memorized, except Jack and the other turkeys. And their lines are super easy, all they have to do is say "gobble" or "bak!" at the right times.

Actually, I take that back how no one except

the turkeys has their lines memorized. Mirisen has all hers memorized perfectly, including all the songs she has to sing. How can she <u>do</u> that? She has the most lines in the entire play! And she's only <u>nine</u>!

When we first started rehearsal, I felt really bad that I didn't have my lines memorized. Over the weekend I tried, I really did. But I just couldn't get it. I didn't feel so bad, though, once the first scene started and everyone was messing up all over the place!

18 days until the play. Only 14 rehearsal days.

<u>May 11</u>

We stink. We're doomed. We're done for! This is what a typical rehearsal sounds like:

Maria (Mirisen): "I'm not kidding. I just saw a turkey—a huge one!—<u>right</u> <u>over</u> <u>there</u>."

John (Keegan): "You mean you're seeing things? Oh wait until Mom and Dad come and—oops, I meant, wait until Mom and Dad find out you're seeing—I mean, no, you're having hallucinations. I mean, you're having elusive—how am I supposed to say it again?"

Mrs. Banks: "illusionations"

John (Keegan): "Right, illusionations."

Katie (me): (great pause) "Oh! It's my line now? Um... excuse me John, I couldn't help overhearing you. Was it possible that you meant—I mean, you thought—I mean, um..."

Mirisen: "that your <u>intention</u>——"

Katie (me): "Oh, yeah. That your intention was to say the word 'hallucinations.' I mean, that your intention was to say the word 'hallucinations'?"

John (Keegan): "Yeah, yeah, whatever."

Me: "You're not supposed to say 'whatever'."

Keegan: "Well, what do I say then? Is this the part where I——"

Mirisen: "You're supposed to say——"

Mrs. Banks (or Mrs. Thera): "Cut! Get your scripts. We can't move on if it's going to be like this."

And it's not just Keegan and me who are terrible. The school scenes are even worse. Sara has a beautiful singing voice and does great on all her solos, but her memory for lines is even worse than mine, and her part is a lot bigger. And there are five other kids who have pretty major parts in the school scenes, and they're just as bad. Oh, and the parts where the bad guys are chasing after the turkeys—forget it!

I have a feeling that this play will go down in history as the worst school play ever.

<u>May 13</u>

Saturday. What a relief! No rehearsal, just time to run through my lines with Mirisen helping me and <u>without</u> Mrs. Banks breathing down my neck. I'm really glad I didn't get the part of Maria now, with how hard this is. I'm also wondering why in the world did Mrs. Banks give me this big of a part? I mean, it's nowhere near as large as Maria or Sarah, or even the turkey catchers or some of the classmates or Mrs. Brett, but it's still pretty big.

I think I finally have the singing part down, or at least I can hear in my head how it's supposed to go. I can sing it at home with just Mirisen, but I feel really nervous singing it in front of my classmates. I keep being afraid I'll mess up. Aaaaa, this is frustrating!

May 16

Mirisen now has not only her entire part, all her lines and songs and everything, memorized, she also has MY entire part memorized! And I think she might have some other kids' parts memorized too, since she's always the one to remind people what they're supposed to say when they forget (which is often).

I got in trouble at school today for making a joke. After Mirisen reminded Tomas (who's playing one of the turkey hunters) of his line for about the hundredth time, I said, "Hey, why don't we just let Mirisen do the whole play? She's memorized everything better than the rest of us have."

Mrs. Banks did <u>not</u> find that funny. She said "Cut!" and had everyone sit down so she could lecture us on the importance of discipline and perseverance and self-control. Almost everyone from both my class and Mrs. Thera's class was glaring at me like it was all my fault. It wasn't! Well, I guess it was, but all I did was make a joke.

May 18

Eight days left. Eight days to turn a disaster into a miracle. I can tell Mrs. Banks and Mrs. Thera are disappointed in us. They do a sixth-grade play every year, but I guess it's never been as bad as this. And it's not like we aren't trying!

I finally have all my lines but one memorized. The one I don't have is a long monologue in which I'm discussing the behavior patterns of turkeys in nature. Did I say it would be <u>easy</u> to act like Katie? It's not. If I were Mirisen, I would probably already know stuff about the behavior patterns of turkeys in nature, but guess what, I'm not so I don't. And I've gotten a little bit better about singing in front of my peers, but I still don't feel entirely comfortable with it. Mrs. Banks still keeps yelling at me to sing more loudly.

Next week we start rehearsing onstage with lighting and costumes. We've already been on the stage since rehearsals started, so we're good with that and <u>most of us</u> know where to go and everything (a few kids are still having difficulties with that, don't ask me why!). But what good are lighting and costumes if half the actors still don't even know what to say at what time?

May 19

Oh my goodness! This might work! Mirisen just came up with the best idea <u>ever</u>. We were rehearsing with Mrs. Thera's class this afternoon, and everybody was messing up as usual. After Nick's fifth time of messing up on his rant about kids' imaginations going wild, he rolled his eyes in frustration and slumped down onto one of the chairs that was set up as a prop. "That's it," he said. "We're never going to be anything more than a school play gone wrong. This is going to be embarrassing."

Mirisen, who had been waiting in the wings for her cue, stared at him. "That's <u>it</u>!" she said. "A school play gone wrong! That should be—we could—I have an idea!"

She ran out onto the stage, and Mrs. Banks frowned. "Mirisen, remember, you have to wait until—"

"I have a great idea!" Everyone's attention was on Mirisen now. It's not often that she comes out and just starts talking over the teacher.

Mrs. Banks didn't look convinced. "Does this idea have something to do with the play, because if not, I'm afraid you're wasting—"

"It does! Listen. A school play gone wrong. We make the title of the play 'A School Play Gone Wrong.'

We add an introduction at the beginning, where it's just the teacher—whoever's playing the teacher, it could be Ashellie since she's the teacher in the play—anyway, the teacher assigns parts, and then the class has to put on this play with barely any notice, and they're really bad! That way, it won't matter if people don't remember their lines, because the 'teacher' can just remind them!"

Mrs. Banks looked confused. So did some of the actors. But I understood what she was trying to say. It wouldn't matter if we messed up, because the entire play was going to be about a class that was messing up. So it would be a play about a class putting on a play.

"Mirisen, this year's play is Turkeys Lurking. If you would like to suggest a different play for next year—"

"No, she's not suggesting a different play," Keegan interrupted. "I think it's a brilliant idea! Cover for our mistakes, and make it seem like we did it that way on purpose. That's awesome!"

A bunch of other kids chimed in that they liked the idea too. Mrs. Banks and Mrs. Thera said they'd have to think about it—Mrs. Thera seemed more in favor of it than Mrs. Banks—but that they'd let us know on Monday. I sure hope they agree to it!

May 22

YES!!!!!!!!! They agreed to it!!!!!! Under one condition:

145

Mirisen is the 'teacher' of the class, and she pretty much has to improvise the entire beginning, where she assigns parts and things. She also gets to say, "Now, since I'm the teacher, I'll get the biggest part," which is really funny! But then, through the rest of it, we pretty much will just run the play, only if anyone forgets their lines, Mirisen can remind them, or—if they're totally lost—she can go and upstage them, just start saying their lines or belting out their songs for them. I think this will be hilarious.

May 25

Yay! We have been doing MUCH better with our "new" play. I think it's funnier than the old one too. We've added in a few parts where we forget our lines on purpose, just so Mirisen can come and do something really crazy instead. And the funny thing is, I really do know all my lines now, I think. It's just nice knowing that I don't <u>have</u> to, and that if I forget, it's okay.

Even though we're doing well, I can't believe TOMORROW is our play! Aaaaaaa! I'm so nervous.

May 26

Yikes yikes yikes!!!!!! In less than 6 hours, I will be performing as Katie in our first performance of our play!!!!!!! Then shortly after that, I'll be performing in the BIG one, in front of all the parents and everyone!!!!!!! I'm so scared.

May 26, later

No need to be scared. We did great!! The kindergarten through fifth grade one was kind of like a dress rehearsal, and we didn't mess up! I mean, a few times people did, but Mirisen was quick to fix that. The kids laughed a LOT at some of Mirisen's improvised lines.

Then we had the one for our parents tonight. They laughed a lot too! I'm so glad Miri came up with that idea. She's such a genius—literally!

After the performance, my family went out for ice cream. I got strawberry, double fudge, and mint chocolate chip. And my parents kept saying what a great job we did. Mirisen's friend Domacie had come too, and while we were eating our ice cream he said that Mirisen did a great job but the rest of us stunk because we couldn't remember our lines. Harrisson just looked at him and said, "Um, Domacie? That's kind of the point." It was a hilarious end to a great night!

Book 10: It's Your Choice

May 30

I'm really excited about Saturday. Mom is taking Mirisen and me on a girls' day out! Girls' days out are really fun. We don't get to have them very often, but when we do, they usually involve ice cream and bookstores and all sorts of other fun stuff. I love going to bookstores with just my mom and sister, because all three of us are huge bookworms and can stay there all day.

June 1

First day of June! Today we got to stay after school for about an hour while Mom did errands. Harrisson played in a little kid area, Pete and Mirisen each went off with friends, and I went into the library and curled up with a book.

Mr. Lebeng summoned us to the office using the PA system around 4:15, and we went and met Mom. Mirisen was really excited about something. She started chatting our ears off as soon as we got outside. "I made a new friend today! It was so cool, because I was hanging out with Michael and Cameron and Emma, and we went to the Snack Shop, and this girl Bobbyn who works there, she's a teenager, she introduced us to her brother Steven! And Steven is exactly one month and five days older than I am, and he's short like me, and he's clumsy like me, and he's _really_ nice! I mean, _really_, we had _so_ much fun together. He goes to our school, too. You know how Michael's there sometimes but is really homeschooled? Well, Steven's not. He _goes_ to Learner's Cove, and he usually stays really late because Bobbyn has to work really late and she's the one who brings him home, so pretty much any time I stay late I'll get to see him! Oh, and he'll be there over the summer too, so we need to come sometime during the summer so I can hang out with him."

Mom nudged me as she and I went over to the left side of the van to get in. "Looks like someone has a new crush."

I giggled. Crush or not, I am glad Mirisen finally has a new friend she's excited about. I mean, she's friends with Michael, but she pretty much only sees him during lunch time. She's friends with Cameron and

Emma, but she sees them even less frequently than she sees Michael. And she's friends with Domacie, but she sees him even less than <u>that</u>. And then she's friends with Carolina, but since Carolina lives in Pennsylvania, they get to see each other even <u>less.</u> So it'll be nice, her having a friend who she can see more often and who goes to our school.

<u>June 3</u>

Girls' Day Out!!! It was <u>super</u> fun. Wait till I get to the best part.

We left around noon and decided to go to the Pheasant Lane Mall. The first place we went in the mall, by unanimous decision, was Borders, the bookstore. Mom held up her cell phone. "I'm setting a timer," she said. "I know that we could all spend all day in here, so I'm setting a timer for one hour. When it goes off, we need to leave Borders and go somewhere else."

"Aww, only an hour?" I protested. "That's too short. How about an hour and a half?"

"One hour and fifteen minutes," Mom decided. "And that's the <u>longest</u> we should be in here!" She went off to the adult section and Miri went to the kids' nonfiction. I spent most of my time in kids' fiction, but made a few trips over to the teen fiction too. Way too soon, the timer went off and we headed to our next destination——the food court!

We ate at Chick-fil-A, which just happens to be my favorite fast food restaurant of all time. We got dessert at Dairy Queen, and then visited the pet store, the toy store, and a fun store called Claire's, which was full of earrings and bracelets and keychains and all sorts of girly stuff. We were poking around at Claire's, just looking at things, when Mom suddenly said, "Hey Allisen, do you want to get your ears pierced?"

I perked up. "Really? I can?"

"Well, as long as you'll be able to take care of them, and as long as you want to, I don't see why not. But it's your choice."

I'd never really thought about getting my ears pierced before, but as I looked around at all the cool earrings they had in the store, I decided it would be super fun to have pierced ears. So my choice was yes.

They had a bunch of earrings near the counter for people who were just getting their ears pierced. I picked out some pretty ones with sapphire, my birthstone. Then I sat in a chair and the lady there gave me a big stuffed mouse to hold onto. She told me to close my eyes, and she warned me that it would probably hurt, but it would be over in a moment. Then she drew dots on my ears where the earrings were going to be, and once I'd looked in the mirror and said they looked good, she pierced my ears. It hurt a LOT at first, but only for a few seconds. Then, she put something cold and wet on my ears, which made them not hurt at all. After that, they felt fine, and I was just so excited to be wearing earrings!!!!!

When we went home, Dad and Harrisson wanted to see my earrings, so I felt kind of like a celebrity. I don't exactly like people looking at me too much or making a big fuss over my appearance, but it was all right. Harrisson just kept asking questions like, "Did it hurt?" and, "Did they actually poke a needle through your <u>ear</u>?" When I told him that they did poke a needle through my ear, he said, "Ewwwww! That's creepy! I don't want to ever get my ears pierced."

"I don't think you'll have to worry about that," I told him.

<u>June 5</u>

I was standing outside of school with Mirisen and Harrisson today, waiting for Mom to pick us up, when I heard a voice behind me. "Hey, Allisen. I have a couple questions for you."

I turned around and saw Jack Bersner. It's funny how I used to hate him but now he's kind of my friend. "Hi Jack," I said.

"Hey. So I have two things to ask—wait, did you just get your ears pierced?"

I nodded, surprised that he had noticed. "Yeah, on Saturday."

"Cool," said Jack. "I want to get one of mine pierced, but my mom won't let me. Anyway, that wasn't one of the things I was going to ask you. I'm gonna be doing a basketball team this summer, at my house, and I was asking kids if they wanna join. It's just an amateur team, you know, and if you have any friends who want to join, you can bring them along too."

"Um..." I said. "Well, I'd have to ask my parents... and I've never really played basketball before..."

"You don't have to be good or anything. It's just for fun. And we don't just play games against each other, we play like HORSE and stuff too. And I want to have us meet twice a week, but you don't have to come to all the meets if you don't want to."

"Uh... hmm, maybe. I'll talk to my mom and let you know." It sounded like it could be fun, but I wasn't sure.

"Okay, great!" Jack smiled. "Oh, and um, my other question. Yeah, so... do you, well, do you maybe want to... go to the end-of-school dance? With me? On the last day of school?"

I had completely forgotten that there was going to be an end-of-school dance. People weren't making such a big deal over it as they had been with the Valentine one. "Well... sure!" I said. "Again, if it's okay with my parents. Yeah, that'd be fun."

Jack gave me a thumbs-up. "Okay. Great. Yeah. Let me know. See you tomorrow!" He moved on, probably to ask more kids if they wanted to join the basketball team.

"I am so glad he came over," said Mirisen. "He reminded me about the dance. I'm going to ask Steven next time I see him if he wants to go to the dance with me!"

June 6

Today is 06-06-06!!!! June 6th, 2006! I love repeating dates. Only 6 more left in this century!

And today I met Steven. We stayed after school, and after we dropped Harrisson off in the little-kid area, Mirisen immediately grabbed my arm and started pulling me along. "Come on, we're going to the Snack Shop, I want you to meet Steven!"

At the Snack Shop was a tall Asian girl who looked like she was in her upper teens. She had long, black hair, and she smiled warmly when she saw us. "Hey! It's Mirisen, right? And is this your sister?"

"Yes," said Mirisen, smiling back. "This is Allisen. Allisen, meet Bobbyn. Bobbyn, meet Allisen. Is Steven here?"

"He should be soon. He usually pops in after he gets out from school."

Sure enough, a few minutes later, a boy came

around the corner. He was only a couple inches taller than Miri, and he had the same black hair and warm smile as his sister. "Hi Mirisen!" he said.

Mirisen grinned. "Steven, this is my sister Allisen. Allisen, this is my friend Steven."

Mirisen, Steven and I hung out at the Snack Shop, just sitting on the stools and talking. Mirisen was right, Steven really was nice, and so was Bobbyn. It wasn't until after we were already home that Miri remembered that she hadn't asked Steven to go to the dance with her.

June 8

"Nooooooo!"

I looked up from the book I was reading in the living room. Mirisen had just hung up the phone, and she looked anguished.

"What's wrong, Miri?" I asked.

"I just got a call from Domacie. He asked me to go to the end-of-school dance with him!"

"So?"

"So... I don't really want to, because I want to go with Steven, but Domacie _asked_ me, so I feel really bad about saying no, especially because Steven and I aren't _technically_ partners yet..."

"You didn't say yes to Domacie, did you?" I asked.

"No, I said I had to go and I'd call him back later,

but now I don't know what to do!"

I didn't see a problem at all. "Just call Steven and ask him to go to the dance with you. Then call Domacie back and say you're already going with someone." I thought of something else. "Hey, how'd Domacie know our school's having a dance anyway?"

She shrugged. "I don't know. But I don't want to hurt Domacie's feelings, and I don't even have Steven's phone number, so I can't do what you suggested."

"Well," I said, "It's your choice, but if it were me, I'd pick Steven."

June 9

I can't believe today is my last day of elementary school. Next year I'll be switching classes and having lots of different teachers and probably tons of homework. I'll miss having this cozy classroom that I stay in all day except for lunchtime and specials.

Today, for the last day of school, we had a party with cupcakes and cookies. When everyone was pretty much done eating, Mrs. Banks had us each write our name on a piece of paper, and pass it around the room, and everybody had to write something nice about each person on the paper with that person's name on it. I wrote "awesome sister, kind, intelligent" on Mirisen's, "fun to hang out with" on Jack's, and "amazing at art" on Rebecca's. Most of the kids in my class were pretty easy, although it was kind of hard to think of something nice for Stivre and Tomas. I ended up writing "very lively" on both of theirs!

It was nice reading mine. Natalia said I was a good singer, Melody said I had a great personality, Jack said I was smart, nice, and talented, and James said I was good at writing. Mirisen wrote "I have known you for nine years, six months, and twenty-four days. You are a wonderful sister and a wonderful friend!"

I talked to my wonderful sister at lunch and asked her if she'd decided about the dance. She hadn't.

June 9, later

Yay! The dance was fun. Mirisen went with Steven!!!!! She went to the Snack Shop after school got out and asked him. He said yes and Bobbyn said that would be fine. I didn't actually see this, but apparently Domacie showed up and tried to get into the dance, but he didn't have a school ID so they didn't let him in. Apparently he was all dressed up in his $200 tux and cologne and everything. Wow.

Anyway, Miri and Steven had fun. And so did Jack and I! We hung out with kids in our class and ate a bunch of snacks, just like last time. He asked me if I'd thought about the basketball thing at all, and to be honest, I hadn't. I asked him to give me his phone number so that I could call him about it.

When I got home, Mom and Dad had some really exciting news! Aunt Brenda and Carolina are coming for a visit in a few days, and they're bringing Mirisen's new gerbils!!! I'm so excited to see them and to meet the gerbils!

June 12

They're here! Aunt Brenda and Carolina and two fuzzy, fluffy gerbils!!!! Yesterday Dad went out and bought a cage for them with all sorts of fun tubes and stuff. And today we got to meet them! They are both brown with cute little faces. Carolina hasn't named them. She said since they're going to be ours, we get to name them.

And guess what! Mirisen named one Gretchen already, after the main character in her favorite fiction book <u>Reaching for the Stars: The Best Is Yet to Come</u>. She said that <u>I</u> can name the other. I have no idea what I want the name to be. I'm feeling a little overwhelmed by all the choices I'm having to make. I still haven't decided about basketball!

June 13

Oh no. I can't <u>believe</u> this! Tomorrow is Mom's 40th birthday and I don't have anything to give her!!! I'm usually really good about remembering people's birth-days, but just with everything that's been going on, it kind of slipped my brain. Now I feel really bad. I don't have a lot of money, and I don't think anyone's going to be able to take me anywhere anyway. Mom likes homemade gifts, so I guess I could write her a little book or something, but no ideas are coming to me right now... maybe I'll call Jack. He was the one who came up with the idea of getting a training collar for Surprise back when she was tearing everything up and Dad was going to bring her back to the pound. Maybe he'll have a good idea about Mom's birthday. And while I'm at it, I'll tell him I'll join his basketball team. Mom said I could if I wanted to. It'll probably be fun, and it'll be a way to get exercise and see kids from school over the summer.

June 13, later

Yay! Jack had a GREAT idea! I found the piece of paper he wrote his number on, and called him. I told him I was planning on joining the team, and he was really excited. He told me when their first meet is going to be (next week). Then I asked him if he had any ideas for Mom's birthday. He said, "Well, you could have a surprise party. You know, invite her friends and stuff, and just surprise her."

How could I not have thought of that?!?!? Mirisen loved the surprise party we threw for her back in November. I think I'm going to tell Mirisen and Carolina about the idea for Mom's birthday (you can't trust

Harrisson with a secret) and we can make decorations and call all of Mom's friends and make a cake somehow. This'll be great!

June 14

TODAY is Mom's birthday. We three girls had an emergency plan meeting in my bedroom last night, while Harrisson was taking a shower. I told them about my idea.

"But Allisen, Mom's birthday is <u>tomorrow.</u> There's no way we're going to be able to call all her friends and get everything set up by then," Mirisen protested.

"Well…" I said. "We can try! Or maybe we can have her party on the weekend or something. I just want to do <u>something</u> special. She's turning <u>forty.</u>"

In the end, we decided that we'd have the party on Saturday (June 17), so we'd have time to call her friends and set up and everything. The other thing we decided was not to tell Dad or Aunt Brenda. Mirisen said we should, but Carolina pointed out that they might not let us have the party if we told them. So they asked me.

"Why do I have to decide?" I complained.

"Because you're the oldest and you'll be the tiebreaker." UGH! Why is everything always my choice?

I thought. Finally I said, "Well… I guess

Carolina's right. We don't want them to say we can't do it."

Tonight worked out fine, because Dad took everyone out to dinner, and when we got home he took a Dairy Queen ice cream cake out of the freezer, and he and Aunt Brenda gave Mom presents. I gave her a card so it wouldn't be suspicious.

Now we just have to wait until Saturday. And call people.

June 16

Yikes! Tomorrow is the party!!!!!! Yesterday, Mirisen, Carolina and I took turns secretly calling all of Mom's friends in the area (Mirisen swiped Mom's address book). We told them that we were having a surprise party for Mom at noon on the 17th, and to try to come and NOT TELL MOM. We also told them not to call us back, because Mom would probably see the caller ID and pick up the phone. It would have been ideal if one of us had a cell phone, so they could call that number, but none of us do, so they're just going to have to come or not come without letting us know which one.

We made decorations today too. We even let Harrisson help us (but we didn't tell him what they were for). The only problem is a cake. We can't just start making one, because everyone would want to know what it was for... we could call one of Mom's friends back and tell them to buy one, but then we'd have to pay them and we don't have a lot of money... so we don't know what to do about that yet.

June 16, later

Yay! Mirisen pointed out that Father's Day is the day after the party, so we can pretend we're making a cake for Father's Day! We asked Mom if we could make a cake today while Dad's at work and she said YES! We told her we didn't want her in the room because "we want it to be a surprise for you too."

Mirisen, Harrisson, Carolina and I made a box chocolate cake and frosted it with both chocolate and vanilla frosting. We wanted to make a Chocolate Cherry Cordial cake from the recipe book—Mom's favorite— but we didn't have any cherries, so we just made plain chocolate. We didn't write on it yet, because we don't want her to see what it's going to say. I am SO excited! But also kind of nervous. Like... what if Mom and Dad had plans for tomorrow? And Carolina and Aunt Brenda are supposed to leave tomorrow night, but what if Aunt Brenda decides to leave earlier? What if Dad gets mad that we didn't tell him? I'm not sure I made the right choice this time.

June 17

The party is today! I'm so nervous...

June 17, later

Wow. The party was... well, let me just tell you about it.

Mirisen, Carolina and I started to get really jumpy around 11 in the morning. We decided to ride bikes so we could immediately see if people were coming. We lowered the seat on Mom's so I could ride it, and we lowered the seat on mine so Carolina could ride it. Then the four of us—Harrisson included—rode up and down the street.

It was 11:47 when the first guest arrived. We immediately put our bikes away and met Mom's best friend, Auntie Diana (she isn't really our aunt but we call her that because she's sort of like an aunt). She stepped out of the car holding balloons and two small presents. "Hi Auntie Diana!" I said. "You're the first one here. I'm going to go get my mom, you keep her out here talking until one of us tells you to come in." Like we'd planned, we kids went in to get Mom. "Auntie Diana's here!" I said. "It looks like she brought a birthday present for you."

"Huh?" said Mom.

"Go outside and look!" I told her.

As soon as Mom was outside, Mirisen and Carolina raced upstairs to get the decorations, and I took the cake down from on top of the refrigerator and took out a tube of pink icing. Then Mirisen carefully wrote "Happy birthday, Mom" in her neat cursive, while Carolina and I taped decorations to the walls and ceiling. Harrisson was really confused. "What are you doing?" he asked. "It was already Mom's birthday."

"I know, but we're having a surprise party for her today," I told him.

We took out a pretty tablecloth and set it on the table. Then we set the cake on the table as well (making sure to keep it in the <u>middle</u>, so Surprise wouldn't get it!). Dad came in and said, "What in the world are you guys doing?"

Mirisen went out to tell Mom to come in, and a minute later, Mom entered, followed by Auntie Diana and another one of her friends, Aunt Elaine. Mom stared around at the decorations. "Is this—what—what is this? What's going on?" She took in the decorations and the cake on the table. "Is this a <u>party</u>?"

"Yes!" exclaimed Carolina. "It's a party for you!"

Nobody noticed at first that Dad and Aunt Brenda looked just as surprised as Mom. Dad immediately offered drinks to the guests (out of our wonderful selection of water, milk, orange juice, and raspberry seltzer), and then started dashing around the kitchen grabbing chips, pretzels, and animal crackers and putting them in bowls.

Everyone hung out and chatted at first, and Mom's friend Renee came over with her husband and a-year-old daughter. By 12:30, we decided that probably no one else was coming, so we had the cake and then Mom opened her presents. The guests stayed until around four, and when everyone was gone, Dad gathered us kids in the living room.

"I don't know what you were thinking, arranging that party without letting any of us know beforehand. I don't even know <u>how</u> you managed to do it, but that's beside the point. You shouldn't have done this without checking with me first."

He was right, and I know the party would've been better if we'd planned it with him (like we would have had more food, and probably better planning. Plus Mom and Dad were kind of upset that we hadn't cleaned up the living room first and there were dirty dishes in the kitchen sink). Dad made us do <u>all</u> the cleanup from the party, which we deserved. But overall, I think everything went well!

<u>June 19</u>

Ayayay. I have another choice to make. Mom found a summer camp online called Camp Nature Woods, and she said that if I want I can go there. It's a Christian camp for kids ages 10-14, and there are all sorts of fun activities like swimming, boating, crafts, and hiking. It sounds like a lot of fun, but here's the thing—it's a sleepover camp, and it's for two whole weeks. I'm not sure if I can take two whole weeks away from my family—what if I get homesick? Or what if they do something really fun without me?

Guess what I haven't done yet. Named the gerbil!!! People keep suggesting names, but nothing sounds exactly right. I want something that goes with the name Mirisen gave the other gerbil. What goes with Gretchen? I have no idea. I have way too much stuff on my mind right now.

June 21

Yesterday was fun! I went over to Jack's house and played basketball. There were a lot of kids from school there—Rob, Mariah, Toby, Nick, Austin, and Stivre, plus three boys from Mrs. Thera's class. Mariah and I were the only girls there, but I was okay with that.

Jack has a basketball court in his backyard. It's not a full-sized one, but it's pretty big and has a net with a backboard and everything. We started by playing Knockout and then we split into two teams and did a little game against each other. I was with Jack, Austin, Brian from Mrs. Thera's class, and Stivre (Jack made the teams). We didn't really keep score, but I think our team won because Jack and Austin both made a ton of baskets! I didn't make any, but that was okay. When we were done playing, Jack's mom brought out a plate of cheese and crackers, some lemonade, and some ice pops. I had a pineapple one. It was fun!

June 25

I have decided to go to camp. It might be scary, and I might miss stuff at home, but it'll be an adventure! I hope I enjoy it. I probably will. It starts on July 10th, so I have from now until then to get ready! I told Jack I wouldn't be able to go to basketball during those two weeks, and he said that was fine and told me to have fun at camp. I sure hope I will!

Oh, and by the way, (I can't believe I didn't write this yet), I named the gerbil. I named her Squeaky, since she squeaks in her cage a lot. Gretchen and Squeaky sound good together, I think.

Okay, I gotta go now. Mom's ready to take me over to Jack's house to play some more basketball!

Book 11: Camp Nature Woods

July 2

Yay! In just 8 days, I will be going to CAMP! It starts on Monday the 10th, and goes until the 24th. Two whole weeks at Camp Nature Woods, sleeping and eating and doing all sorts of activities with a bunch of other kids ages 10-14. There are over 200 acres of woods, plus a big lake and lots of cabins and a lodge where we eat. It's going to be awesome! I'm going to learn so many new things! I can't wait!

July 4

Today is Independence Day. Later tonight, my family and I are going to go to Holman Stadium to watch the fireworks. Even Pete might end up coming. He likes the Fourth of July because he gets to see things blow up in the sky (Of course, he'd probably rather shoot off his <u>own</u> fireworks). He probably won't come with us, though, which I'm glad about.

July 4, later

Wow. The fireworks were spectacular! I love fireworks! I don't know if Pete came or not (he was over at a friend's house when we left and we didn't see him at the stadium), but the rest of us sure had fun! My favorites were the ones that were heart-shaped and the ones that spelled out U.S.A.

After we watched that cool show, we went to Dairy Queen. Mom and I split a strawberry-banana Blizzard, Dad and Harrisson got chocolate-dipped cones, and Mirisen got a strawberry sundae. Yum yum!

July 7

Oh my goodness. In three days I'll be at camp! I'm excited, but also kind of nervous. Two whole weeks away from my family? I hope I don't get homesick or scared. I hope my family doesn't go out to dinner or bowling or anything else fun without me. I hope I <u>like</u> camp. What if I don't like it?

Okay, I should stop worrying. I'm sure it'll be just fine. I'm going to go start packing now.

July 9

Yikes! I'm leaving TOMORROW! Everything is all

packed up. We'll be leaving at 9:30 tomorrow morning because camp starts at noon and it takes two hours to get there, and Mom wants to make sure I'm on time. I'm bringing all my shorts (7 pairs), 4 pairs of long pants, 10 T-shirts, two sweatshirts, all my socks and underwear, my two bathing suits, a hat, some sunscreen, 6 towels, my toothbrush, toothpaste, bug spray, 7 ponytail holders, three pens, two books, some stationery, my favorite stuffed elephant Nosey, and of course this diary! Oh, and the ear-cleaning antiseptic I got last month when I got my ears pierced. Mom said I probably don't need to bring so many clothes, since they'll have laundry facilities available. But I'm not taking any chances.

Only 19 hours until I leave!

July 10

I am at camp. Mom dropped me off about ten hours ago. There were a bunch of other kids around, talking and hugging their family members. Mom and I hugged for a long time before she left. I almost cried when she drove away, knowing I won't see her for two weeks. But I held it in and just looked around at my surroundings. I could see a cabin in the distance, and lots and lots of trees.

"This is crazy, isn't it?" said a girl near me. She looked to be a little older than me. I nodded.

"This your first time at camp?" the girl asked.

I nodded again.

"Mine too," she said. "I went to swim camp last summer, but that was just a day camp. And I've been on overnights before with my church's youth group, but those are only a couple days. So this two week thing is kind of intimidating."

"Yeah," I agreed. "I've never been away from my family overnight at all."

"Wow," said the girl. "I hope you don't get homesick. I hope I don't get homesick either, actually. Hey, I just realized something. I don't know your name. I'm Kiana. What's your name?"

"I'm Allisen." I liked Kiana. She reminded me of Emalie Maye— really talkative and outgoing and everything.

"I like that name. Nice to meet you, Allisen."

I talked with Kiana until the camp directors called us to follow them to the dining hall for lunch.

Lunch was chicken patties, a bun, salad, fruit, and a cookie. We were all assigned randomly to different tables, so I wasn't with Kiana. There was a bucket in the middle of the table which the counselors said was the Yuck Bucket. The Yuck Bucket was where we had to pour all our leftover scraps from our plates. The counselors told us that whichever table had the least Yuck would win a prize, such as not having to clean up.

I made sure to eat everything on my plate.

After lunch, we were assigned to our cabins. I was kind of hoping I'd be with Kiana, since she was the only person I knew at the camp. But we were assigned by our ages, and Kiana was thirteen. I ended up in Cabin G113. A counselor explained that G is for Girls, 11 is for the age 11, and 3 is because it's the third — and last — cabin for 11-year-old girls (They sort us alphabetically by last names).

I'm not sure how I feel about my cabin-mates. There are five of them aside from me. Their names are Endri, Lauren, Milly, Beth, and Tabitha. I don't know any of them, but Lauren, Beth, Milly, and Tabitha all know each other. Lauren and Beth are best friends who don't like Tabitha and Milly, and Tabitha and Milly are best friends who don't like Beth and Lauren. And then there's Endri, who seems just kind of mean and bossy. She immediately claimed the top bunk near the window and sprawled her stuff out all over the bottom bunk as well. Milly and Tabitha claimed one of the other bunk beds, and Lauren and Beth claimed the only one left, so guess who was left with the bunk under Endri's? That's right. Me.

"Hey, um, Endri?" I asked. "Can you move your stuff?"

"Just a minute," she said. A "minute" took more like half an hour. By the time I finally got to set up my bed with my pillow and blankets and Nosey, it was time for the opening ceremony.

I'm not going to write much about the opening ceremony because it was kind of boring—they just went over camp rules and stuff. When the ceremony was done, we had dinner, and then they gave us a little bit of time in the game room, with ping pong tables and foosball and things. Tomorrow we get to do more outside stuff. I can't wait!

July 12

Yesterday we did some hiking, and looked for animal tracks in the dirt. It's too bad Mirisen isn't here, because she would have <u>loved</u> it. The counselors showed us how to recognize whether the tracks were from deer, bears, dogs, raccoons, or squirrels. We found some of each of those, except bear tracks, and we even found some other tracks that the counselors thought might belong to a skunk, but they weren't sure. I hope if it is a skunk, it stays away from all of us!

We did crafts after the hike, in the craft house. It was pretty cool. We made fake animal prints in clay, trying to make them look as much like the real animal tracks as we could. I made mine raccoon tracks.

Today, we did an all day hike. This was awesome for several reasons: 1. I like hiking. 2. I like nature and learning the names of the different trees and flowers. 3.

I like being outside. 4. I like being out of that cabin with those annoying girls!

My cabin-mates are driving me crazy. Last night, Lauren and Beth stayed up all night talking, and Milly and Tabitha kept saying, "Be QUIET!" and finally Endri came back from her 45-minute trip to the bathroom (which is in a separate building, kind of in the middle of all the cabins) and said, "Everyone be quiet. I need my sleep." (except she actually said it in a much ruder way). Beth and Lauren kept talking and then Endri started yelling and I just put my pillow over my head and tried to get some sleep. It was awful.

July 13

Yay! Today we get to go swimming in the lake! I was wondering when we would get to. I saw the lake when I first arrived, and it looked really nice. Pretty large, with a free swim area near the shore, and then a deeper swim area that has a dock with a rope swing and diving board on it. I'm <u>really</u> interested in trying those out.

July 13, later

As it turned out, everyone had to take a swimming test before they could use the diving board or rope swing. That was no problem for me, because I'm a good swimmer. I passed the test easily and spent most of the day on the rope swing. It's so fun to swing on that and then just let go and land in the water! I've never done anything like that before.

After swimming, we all gathered around in a big circle and played catch with several balls going at once, in all different directions, and you had to try not to let any of them hit the ground. It was fun, and it made me wish Harrisson was here because he would have loved it.

July 15

You know, camp is fun and everything, but sometimes I wish I was back at home. Nights are the worst. During the day I have activities to keep me occupied, but at night all I can do is listen to my cabin-mates argue and think about how much I miss my family.

I miss having my mom come in and kiss me good night when I go to bed. I miss having Sniffer snuggle up with me and purr me to sleep every night. I miss my room and my comfy bed. The beds here are <u>not</u> comfortable. I miss my parents and Surprise and the cats and the gerbils. I even miss Harrisson begging me to play and Mirisen correcting my grammar! The only one I don't miss is Pete... well, okay, maybe I even miss <u>him</u> a little bit! Wow, this is really awful. Just <u>thinking</u> about home makes me sad. And I don't even have any good friends here, because most of the other kids have made friends from their own cabins, and...well, let's just say that definitely hasn't happened for me. I don't like <u>anyone</u> in my cabin. I'm soooooooooo lonely.

July 17

Today I got a letter from my family, saying they missed me and they hoped I was having fun at camp and why hadn't I written them any letters? I'm going to try to write one now, even though my head hurts and I'm tired. That's another thing I don't like about camp: we have to get up at 7 every morning! I am not a morning person. And we usually have late-night activities—singing and worship time mostly, which are fun but make it so that we don't even get back to our cabins until 10. And then lights-out isn't until 11, and I usually can't get to sleep until at least 12, because of all the noise. I wish I could switch cabins.

July 18

"Hey everyone, I have a great idea. Let's have a sneak swim in the lake." That was Endri, last night. It was after lights-out, but of course Lauren and Beth were still talking and Milly and Tabitha kept telling them to be quiet and Endri had just come in again from one of her insanely long trips to the "bathroom."

"What?" said Milly, incredulously. "Are you kidding?

We'd get in so much trouble! It's like 11:30! Nobody's supposed to be out at this time. Even the <u>counselors</u> are in bed."

"I know!" said Endri, grinning. "That's why it's fun!"

"It's not fun to do stuff you're not allowed to do," Tabitha said softly.

Endri made a disgusted noise. "What are you guys, babies?" she taunted.

"<u>We're</u> not babies," Beth said, speaking for herself and Lauren. "<u>We'll</u> come with you."

"You guys are so dumb," said Milly. "Didn't you hear what the counselors said, that if you're caught swimming after dark or sneaking around after lights-out, you get sent home?"

"Yeah, but no one's going to catch us," said Endri. "Come on, guys. It'll be awesome!"

Lauren and Beth were already getting out of bed. "You scaredy-cats aren't coming?" Endri asked Milly and Tabitha.

"No way," said Milly. "We're not scared, just smart. <u>We</u> don't want to get sent home."

"Whatever. Suit yourself. What about invisible girl?" Suddenly, a flashlight was shining in my face. I pretended to be asleep. "You coming, invisible girl? Tell you what. You come, and you can be my friend. We'll hang out together tomorrow and for the rest of camp. Then you'll have someone to hang out with and you won't be so miserable."

Was it really that obvious? And why was she calling me invisible? Because I'm quiet and don't really associate with anyone from the cabin? Not like I really cared. I didn't want Endri as a friend. I kept pretending to be asleep.

"I bet she's faking," I heard Lauren's voice. "Tabitha and Milly were being really loud."

Tabitha and Milly immediately began protesting that they were only being loud to tell Beth and Lauren to be quiet.

"Guys, it doesn't matter!" said Endri. "Although... I have a great idea. What if we do something to her while she's sleeping? Anyone have any hair gel? Or shaving cream?"

I considered letting them do stuff to me, and then I could just go to the counselors' cabin next door and tell on them. But that might not work out so well. I opened my eyes.

"I'm awake," I said. "I heard everything you guys were talking about. And I'm not sneaking down to the lake. Milly and Tabitha are right. You guys are just going to get in trouble."

Endri, Lauren, and Beth rolled their eyes, and I noticed they looked a little disappointed that they weren't going to get to "do" anything to me. "Fine," said Endri. "Lauren, Beth, let's go."

The three of them left the cabin. A few minutes later, Tabitha said, "This is <u>great</u>!"

"I know," said Milly. "They are so outta here!" I heard them both getting up.

"We're going to go tell the counselors what they're doing," Tabitha said to me. "You wanna come with us?"

I didn't really want to get involved. I just wanted to get some sleep.

Milly and Tabitha left, and I actually did fall asleep and didn't wake up until 7. But I found out in the morning what had happened—Endri, Lauren and Beth really did get sent home from camp. The counselors said they'll be switching a new girl into our cabin to even out the numbers in the cabins. Personally, I'd be fine keeping it just the three of us—at least I'd be able to get some sleep! Maybe camp will be a little bit better now.

<u>July 18, later</u>

The new girl in our cabin is named Lindie. She transferred from G112. She seems nice. She took Lauren's old top bunk, and walked next to me to the dining hall for dinner. We talked on the way and she said she didn't mind moving to a new cabin because she was kind of the odd one out in her old cabin. Sound familiar?

We weren't assigned to the same table for

supper, but we talked on the way to worship time. Lindie has three little brothers and a little sister, and four cats and two dogs. She lives up in Maine and goes to a small Christian school, where there were only 9 kids in the entire 6th grade last year! She likes to read, write, swim, do crafts, spend time with her family, and sing songs. She has a best friend, but her best friend moved to Montana last year. And she keeps a journal! She is so much like me it's creepy. I think we are going to become friends.

July 20

Yesterday was super fun, because I did everything with Lindie.

First, everybody went on a hike, and we got to try two dandelion foods—dandelion pancakes and fried dandelions. Lindie and I both didn't like the fried dandelions that much, but we agreed that the pancakes tasted normal.

Lindie and I made sure we were in a group together for the team-building activity we did when we got back from the hike, and then went swimming during free choice time. We each took a few turns on the rope swing and then decided to try going together, but that didn't work out so well because our knees knocked together and we both ended up getting gobfuls of water up our noses.

We sat next to each other during worship time, and Lindie showed me a couple sign language signs she knew that went along with some of the songs we sang. When we got back to the cabin, Lindie asked if I wanted to switch to the top bunk (that used to be Endri's) or the bottom bunk beneath hers (the one that was Beth's) so we could talk better. I moved my stuff to Endri's old bed, but then I ended up bringing Nosey over to Lindie's so we could play with stuffed animals together. Lindie had brought a horse named Terra and a cat named Callie.

Lindie and I played and whispered and giggled on Lindie's bunk until Tabitha and Milly said, "Be QUIET!" and then I climbed over to my new bed—without touching the ground, just right from Lindie's to mine—and we went to sleep.

July 20, later

Guess what we got to do today! We went CANOEING! Lindie and I got to go in the same canoe. The counselors taught us how to paddle, and how to turn and everything. It was actually harder than I expected it to be, because everyone had to work together to get it to turn the right way. We all had to pay attention to what other people were doing, making sure we were paddling at the same rate and everything. Also, by the time we were done, my arms were SORE! It was quite a workout!

We canoed pretty far out into the lake, then turned around and went back toward shore. When we reached the swimming area, the counselors told us to all lean to one side and let the canoe tip over! That was fun. Then we had to go under the upside-down canoe and work together to flip it back over. Lindie and I had a private conversation under ours!

We spent the rest of the day relaxing in the game room and the crafts lodge. A little later, we had a team-building activity outside, where we had to figure out how to make a human pyramid without anyone talking. <u>That</u> was interesting! Then, after dinner, we had worship time <u>outside</u>, around a big campfire, and we sang songs and roasted marshmallows. It was great—and the best part was that I had a friend to share it with.

<u>July 23</u>

Oh my goodness. Time really does fly when you're having fun! Tomorrow is my LAST day of camp!

The 21st was rainy. So was today. Actually, right now, it's 10:06 at night, and there is a huge storm going on outside. Lindie and I are writing in our journals. Today (as well as the 21st) we did crafts and some indoor team-building activities. Yesterday we had a whole-camp Capture the Flag game, which was really fun! There were four teams, and Lindie and I were on the same team. Our team didn't win, but it was still a lot of fun.

Tomorrow we'll have a closing ceremony and about an hour of free time before our parents will start coming to pick us up. I hope it's nice out so Lindie and I can go swimming! Camp has been a lot of fun. But I'm also really excited about getting to see my family tomorrow.

Ooh, Lindie's done writing in her journal. I'm going to stop writing so I can do something with her!

July 24

Home again, home again! It feels so good to be home. And to see my family again!!!!!!!!!!!

It was sunny for my last day of camp. I didn't even mind getting up at 7, because I knew we only had a few more hours before the end of camp.

The counselors let us sit wherever we wanted for breakfast today. I sat with Lindie and some of the kids who had been on our team for Capture the Flag. We had the closing ceremony and a short worship service where we sang some of the songs we'd been singing for the past two weeks. Then from 10-11 we had free time, and Lindie and I raced down to the lake and went off the rope swing a bunch of times. Free time was over way too soon. Cabin clean-up time was next, when we got our cabins spotless and packed up all our stuff. And then it was time to say goodbye.

We gathered to wait for our parents in the same area we'd been dropped off. It was actually quite a lot like when we'd been dropped off, because it was a bunch of kids with suitcases and everything. Except this time, everyone was reliving camp memories and hugging their friends and crying about how much they were going to miss each other.

I saw Kiana through the crowd. "Come on," I said to Lindie. "I want to talk to someone." We'd been separated by age for most of the camp activities, so I hadn't really seen Kiana much except at worship time and during meals. We hadn't been near each other during most worship times, and we'd only been at the same table for two meals.

"Hey," I said to her. "Remember me?"

Kiana turned away from the group of friends she was chatting with. When she saw me, she smiled. "Yeah! Allisen, right? How'd you end up liking camp?"

"It was good," I told her. "And this is my new friend Lindie. Lindie, this is Kiana."

Lindie and I hung out with Kiana and her friends until Kiana's mom came to pick her up. And just a few minutes later, my family arrived.

"Allisen!!!!!" Harrisson came running to greet me. He jumped into my arms and I swung him around. "I missed you so much!" he exclaimed.

Mom, Dad, and Mirisen came and covered me with hugs. "Are you hungry?" Dad asked me.

"Daddy said we get to go to Olive Garden!" exclaimed Harrisson. "Ready to go?"

Almost.

I gave Lindie a looooong hug. "I'm really glad you got switched to my cabin," I told her.

"Me too!" she agreed. "It was so much fun hanging out with you every day."

Lindie and I exchanged addresses and phone numbers, and promised to write and call each other. I knew she was a friend I'd never lose.

My family did go out to eat at Olive Garden, and I told them all about camp. What we did every day, what I learned about plants and trees and animals, what the food was like, what the weather was like, and of course about all my cabin-mates and hanging out with Lindie. "Lindie seems like a nice girl," Mom said. "Where does she live again? Maybe we can see about you two getting together sometime."

When we got home, Surprise greeted me with lots of crazy jumping and licking and tail-wagging. Sniffer came up and rubbed against my legs, purring. Tuxio and Leelee came out to greet me as well, and even Pete gave me a half-smile and a "Welcome back," when he came home from wherever he'd been. I just ran around the house, smiling at all the familiar smells and sights and sounds, and then went into my room, where I marveled at everything familiar.

Now I am sitting in my very own comfy bed, with Sniffer curled up in a fluffy ball next to me. Camp was a lot of fun—maybe I'll go next year too. Maybe Mirisen will come with me, since she'll be 10 by then. Hopefully Lindie will be there too. But for now, I'm happy to be home. There's no place like home.

Home sweet home.

Book 12: Do You See How I See?

July 28

Wow, I don't know what's gotten into me lately. My head's been hurting a lot, and I feel like I'm getting tired more than usual too. Maybe I'm still trying to make up for all the sleep I lost when I was at camp for two weeks. Maybe I'll be better soon. I hope I don't have any kind of disease.

July 30

I'm seriously starting to think something's wrong with me. I love to read. Usually. But we went to the library yesterday, and I checked out a bunch of books, and I barely got through the third chapter of the first one I started. Not because it wasn't interesting—it was the newest book in my favorite series, so I was dying to read it! But after even the first few pages, my head was pounding again and my vision was starting to get blurry. I tried holding the book really close to my face, really far away from my face... each time, I'd be able to read for about a page, and then that strategy wouldn't work anymore and I'd have to try something new. Now my head is pounding again. I'm going to go lie down.

August 2

A new kid lives in our neighborhood now. His name is David Miksi, and he's seven, just like Harrisson. Harrisson's really excited. We've never had any friends in our neighborhood before.

David came over to our house today—well, really our yard. He and Harrisson played on the swings and then Mirisen and I joined them in the front yard for a game of Wiffle ball. We played girls against boys. And even though the boys were younger, they smoked us.

Mirisen is awful at sports. Not to insult her or anything, but she just is. The thing is, though, I'm usually pretty good at sports. I'm not an athlete or anything, but I can usually at least hit the ball when it's thrown to me. I don't know what got into me today. I couldn't hit anything. Of course, maybe the problem was that I had a hard time <u>seeing</u> the ball as it came toward me. Whose idea was it to make Wiffle balls white, anyway? They should be like neon pink.

When it was our turn to pitch and outfield, we also stunk. I was all right at pitching, but then Harrisson or David would hit the ball and I'd be looking around, trying to see where it went, and Miri would be yelling, "It went right past you! Go get it!" It was not very enjoyable.

And nor is this headache. Good bye. I'm going to sleep.

August 5

Noooooooooo! The symptoms are just getting worse and worse. I don't even know what they're symptoms <u>of</u>. What disease makes people have headaches, blurry vision, and not be able to read or write for long periods of time? I'm kind of afraid to find out.

Maybe I'll look up my symptoms on the computer sometime. The only problem is, I think stuff you look up on the computer can be traced, and I don't want anyone in my family seeing what I'm looking up. I don't want to worry them. Because, I mean, it may not be something bad. It probably isn't. And if it isn't, I'd feel pretty ridiculous having my family find out that I'm all worried over nothing. And if it is something bad... well, I don't want them to know yet. I don't even want to know yet.

Maybe I won't look anything up on the computer.

August 6

This is interesting news. Later this month, my cousins from California are going to be coming to visit us!!! I'm excited. I haven't seen them in a long time. I just hope my symptoms have stopped by then... and I hope I haven't found out that I have some terrible disease by then. Maybe I'll wait until after they leave before I mention anything.

August 8

This disease or whatever is really messing everything up. I went to Jack's house for basketball today, and just like with Wiffle ball in our yard, I was awful. At least I could <u>see</u> the ball this time (it's kind of hard to miss a big orange basketball), but it was a little hard to tell sometimes who was on my team and who wasn't. I actually passed to people on the other team a couple times! And shooting—forget it. I tried for two baskets and I made zero.

I just had a terrifying thought. What if I'm

going blind?

August 12

I think maybe I am going blind. I'm so scared. I can't even imagine what that would be like, to not be able to see at all. I am very thankful that nobody I know is blind or deaf, because I would just feel so bad for them. Imagine being both, like Helen Keller! That would be so terrible. Or imagine having <u>no</u> senses! That would be the <u>worst</u>. You couldn't do <u>anything</u>, not even think, because even deaf and blind people think in smells, tastes, and feelings.

I'm really freaking myself out by thinking about having no senses. I'm really glad I have all my senses working properly.

For now.

August 14

I can't take it anymore. I think I'm going to tell someone. Probably my mom. I've been trying to hide it, but I just can't anymore. I played horribly at basketball again yesterday. I tried reading a book out loud to Harrisson last night, and I had to really strain to see the words on the page. Today I tried to read back on some of my old diary entries, and I could barely read some of the earlier ones, and I noticed that I've started writing bigger and bigger just so I can see what I'm writing.

I'm sooooo scared. I kind of feel like as soon as I tell Mom she'll go, "Oh no! I know what that is! It's cancer!" or something else just as bad. But I really think I have to tell her.

August 14, later

Oh, I am soooooooooooooooo relieved! Well, pretty much. After dinner, I stayed with Mom in the kitchen while she washed dishes. Dad had gone outside with Surprise, and Mirisen and Harrisson had gone to their room to play, so it was just Mom and me.

"Mom?" I said, gathering up my courage.

"Yes?" she said.

"Um... well, I... it's really annoying. Every time I try to read or write, my head hurts."

"Your head hurts?"

"Yeah. And, like, my vision kind of gets blurry... and I sort of have trouble seeing some stuff. Like when I go over to Jack's house to play basketball."

Mom looked at me for a moment. "I think I'll schedule you an appointment with my eye doctor," she said. "I remember having those same things happen to me when I was in college. That was when I found out I needed glasses. It might be time to get you glasses."

At first I was tremendously relieved. Glasses? That's it? I'm not dying or anything? But then... I don't know. I mean, I'd certainly rather have glasses than cancer. But... glasses! I never really thought I'd have to wear them, I guess. It'll be weird.

Well, I'll try to focus on the positive. At least I don't have any terrible disease (I'm pretty sure!). Mom is going to schedule me an appointment and then I'll find out for sure.

August 16

I'm really nervous. My appointment is today! I'll find out what's wrong with me, I guess...

August 16, later

Wow! I can see perfectly well now. It's amazing

how clear my vision is. I am now wearing my brand-new glasses.

Mom took me to her ophthalmologist (I had to ask Mom how to spell that!). That's a long fancy word meaning "eye doctor." The eye doctor had me go through a bunch of those eye charts—you know, the ones with the big E on top, and then a bunch of other smaller letters. I easily read the first few lines, but then the letters started blurring into a fuzzy mess. Then the doctor had me cover one eye while he moved his hand and asked if I could see it in different positions. Then he did that same thing with a pen, making me follow the movement of the pen with my eyes. He had me look through something where it showed different images in the left and right eye, and asked me which image was clearer. And <u>then</u> he had me stare at a painting on the wall as he covered and uncovered each of my eyes in turn. He also did stuff like putting fluids in my eyes, which just made my vision blurrier, and flashing lights in my eyes and studying what was happening. The whole time I was just thinking about how people always say "don't stare at the sun," and wondering if he was trying to damage my eyes on purpose so he'd be able to sell me glasses.

"Well," he concluded after he'd done everything. "It doesn't look like you're at risk for any eye diseases. However, what you do have is astigmatism."

I stared at him. "Is that bad?" I asked. I had never heard that word before and it sure sounded like a disease to me.

"All it means is that you'll need glasses," he told me. "Ordinary old everyday glasses. Astigmatism means that the way your eyes are curved distorts the way you see things."

He explained some other stuff to Mom and me, mainly to Mom. Then we went out to the waiting room and I got to pick out which frames I wanted for my glasses. It took a while—did I want sleek rectangular ones like Mom's? Did I want round ones? Square ones? Finally I selected a set of large pinkish frames that were kind of a mix between round and square. The doctor put the correct kind of lenses in them and then gave me the glasses to put on.

It was amazing. As soon as I put the glasses on, I could SEE! I mean, I thought I'd been seeing all along. But I guess I never realized how blurry my vision really was until I saw what everything looked like without the blurriness. Everything was so crystal clear and perfect. I guess my vision's been bad for a long time without me even knowing it.

Now I am writing in my journal without getting the slightest headache. I look weird with glasses. When Mom and I got home, Dad, Mirisen, and Harrisson were all exclaiming over my new glasses and all that stuff, and all I wanted to do was just go be by myself. I don't like getting that kind of attention.

Oh NO! I just realized something! When I go back to school in September... are kids going to be exclaiming over my glasses? Will they think I look weird? Will they even recognize me?

August 18

I love my new glasses because I can see so well out of them. But I hate them for other reasons.

Like the fact that I have to wear them EVERY SINGLE DAY, ALL DAY, FOR EVER!!!!!!!!!! They are <u>so</u> uncomfortable on the bridge of my nose and on my ears. I'm not used to them yet. I can only take them off while I'm sleeping and when I'm in the shower. And when I do take them off, everything blurs up again. Oh, and yesterday, I was playing a sort of soccer game with Harrisson and David, and my glasses <u>fell</u> <u>off</u>. I almost stepped on them!

I'm not going to be able to deal with this for the rest of my life. I'm not looking forward to basketball tomorrow AT ALL. Maybe I just won't go.

August 19

Mom made me go to basketball. I said I just didn't feel like playing, but she knew my real reason. "Allisen, you're going to have glasses for the rest of your life, or at least until you're old enough to wear contact lenses. You can't just hide away and not do stuff because you're wearing glasses."

So she drove me over to Jack's house. Jack and five other kids from school were already in the backyard basketball court, warming up. "I don't think I'll be able to play basketball," I told Mom. "What if the ball hits me in the face?"

"Has the ball ever hit you in the face before?"

"Um... no, but... what if someone elbows me and my glasses fall off and someone steps on them?"

Mom told me to stop worrying. Then Jack saw me and came over. "Hey, Allisen. I like your glasses. Are they new?"

I nodded. "I got them three days ago."

"So can you see a lot better now? Did you have trouble seeing before?"

I nodded again. We went down and joined the rest of the group for basketball. Nobody else mentioned my glasses. We played HORSE, and I didn't get hit in the face. We played Knockout and Toby came close to knocking off my glasses, but he didn't. We had a short scrimmage and once my glasses got kind of crunched into my face, but they didn't break and it didn't really hurt. And my glasses didn't fall off at all.

I feel a little bit better about playing basketball now, but still... I wish I didn't have to wear glasses!

August 20

Cousins coming tomorrow! I'm so excited. I hope they're nice. I hope they haven't seen pictures of me without my glasses and go, "Hey, who's that?" when they see me.

August 21

The cousins are here! The cousins are: Nina, age four, who's tiny and whiny and stays with her mother (my Aunt Madison) all the time; Linna, age eight, who's spunky and full of energy and runs all over the place and bounces off the walls; and Jonathan, age fourteen, who... wears glasses!!!!!!!!!!!!

I asked Jonathan about his glasses during dinner tonight. He said he's been wearing glasses since he was nine. "Aren't they annoying?" I asked him.

He thought about that. "Not really anymore," he said. "I remember when I first got them I hated them. I thought they were really uncomfortable, and I kept forgetting them and leaving them places, and I thought all the kids at school were going to make fun of me because I was the <u>only</u> kid in my fourth grade class with glasses. Oh, and I broke them once, hanging upside down on the monkey bars. They fell off my head and some kid stepped on them and they snapped right down the middle. I thought my mom and dad were going to kill me."

"But you don't mind them now?" I asked.

"Honestly, I'm so used to them now, it feels weird when I <u>don't</u> wear them. They're just like... part of me, sort of. And now when kids see me without my glasses, they're like, 'Whoa, <u>that's</u> what you look like without glasses? That's so weird!'"

Well, if Jonathan can get used to wearing glasses, then I can too. I just hope it doesn't take <u>long</u> for me for get used to them.

<u>August 24</u>

The cousins are leaving tomorrow. We've been having fun together. It's weird, because when we're with Carolina's family, all of us kids usually hang out together. But with these cousins, it's like we're split up into groups. Harrisson and Linna hang out together all the time, tearing around the house pretending to be racecars or something. Mirisen plays things like dolls and stuffed animals with Nina. Jonathan sometimes hangs out with the adults and sometimes with me. When he's hanging out with me, we like ride bikes (he rides Dad's), or play catch, or talk about school and books and movies. We've both read Harry Potter, so we talk about that a lot. And then sometimes we both just sit with the grownups and listen as they talk about us.

Today I asked Jonathan if he wanted to come over to Jack's house and play basketball with the group.

He said that sounded fun. So Mom drove both of us over, and I introduced my cousin to Jack and all the other kids.

When we split into teams to do a scrimmage, Jonathan was on my team, and we <u>flattened</u> the other team. I think that probably had to do with the fact that Jonathan is two years older and quite a bit taller than everyone else, plus he plays basketball for his school team, so he's really good.

Jonathan told me that he has a special glasses band for when he plays sports, so his glasses don't fall off. I wonder if I can get one of those.

<u>August 25</u>

I've had my glasses for one week and two days. And I'm sort of getting used to them, I guess. They're still kind of uncomfortable, but only when I really think about them. And it's still a little weird when I look in the mirror, but not <u>that</u> weird.

I'll be starting school on September 6. <u>Middle</u> school. That's so weird. I wonder what it'll be like. I hope I have friends in my classes. I hope the teachers are nice and the work isn't too hard. I hope I don't get confused with all the switching of classes!

Well, no need to worry about that right now. I've still got almost two weeks left of summer, and I'm going to enjoy them!

About the Author

Kelsey Gallant originally started writing the Allisen's Notebooks series when she was eleven years old, using 3-4 sheets of folded printer paper to make each of her small, illustrated books. Each original book was later typed and edited into its current form as a chapter in *6th Grade With My Crazy Classmates, My Super Smart Sister, & Me*, which was first published shortly after Kelsey turned twenty-one.

Like Allisen, Kelsey enjoys reading, drawing, swimming, being outside, and (of course) writing. She does not have a super-smart little sister or a crazy older brother, but she does have two wonderful younger brothers who she enjoys spending time with. Kelsey lives with her family in Nashua, New Hampshire.

Other Books by Kelsey Gallant

Allisen's Notebooks 2:

7th Grade With My Fabulous Friends, My New Neighbors, & Me

Allisen's Notebooks 3:

8th Grade With My Awesome Adventures, My Various Visitors, & Me

I Didn't Plan This

Alanna is upset when things start changing at the beginning of seventh grade. But is it possible that some changes are for the better?

Don't miss these super special e-shorts!

Each is between 6,000 and 12,000 words long, and focuses on a month in the life of one of Allisen's siblings or friends. Get the inside scoop on their lives and hear about Allisen from a new perspective!

Available on Amazon.com

Are you interested in more of Allisen? Check out my website,

KelseyGallant.com!

You'll find updates on the newest installments in the series, answers to the questions you may have, and exclusive author notes about all the books. You can also learn about my other novels and short stories, and explore my "Teen Talk" section—opinions and advice for teenagers on relevant topics.

You can also find me on Facebook **(Facebook.com/officialkelseygallant)**

or send me an email at **kelseygallant18@gmail.com!**

Made in the USA
Las Vegas, NV
23 May 2023

72474462R00132